MARY ANNE AND THE
MEMORY GARDEN

**Other books by
Ann M. Martin**

Rachel Parker, Kindergarten Show-off
Eleven Kids, One Summer
Ma and Pa Dracula
Yours Turly, Shirley
Ten Kids, No Pets
Slam Book
Just a Summer Romance
Missing Since Monday
With You and Without You
Me and Katie (the Pest)
Stage Fright
Inside Out
Bummer Summer

BABY-SITTERS LITTLE SISTER series
THE BABY-SITTERS CLUB mysteries
THE BABY-SITTERS CLUB series
(See back of book for a more complete listing.)

MARY ANNE AND THE MEMORY GARDEN

Ann M. Martin

AN
APPLE
PAPERBACK

SCHOLASTIC INC.
New York Toronto London Auckland Sydney

No part of this publication may be reproduced in whole or in part, or stored in a retrieval system, or transmitted in any form or by any means, electronic, mechanical, photocopying, recording, or otherwise, without written permission of the publisher. For information regarding permission, write to Scholastic Inc., 555 Broadway, New York, NY 10012.

ISBN 0-590-22877-3

12 11 10 9 8 7 6 5 4 3 2 1   6 7 8 9/9 0 1/0

Printed in the U.S.A.   40

First Scholastic printing, January 1996

The author gratefully acknowledges
Jahnna Beecham
and
Malcolm Hillgartner
for their help in
preparing this manuscript.

MARY ANNE AND THE
MEMORY GARDEN

CHAPTER 1

"Deck the halls with boughs of holly, fa-la-la-la, la-la-la-la!"

Sharon was singing so loudly that Tigger, my gray-striped kitten, bolted out of the kitchen into our living room. He leaped into my lap and buried his little head under my arm to shut out the noise.

Why was my stepmother singing Christmas carols in January? Partly because they're some of the few songs to which she (sort of) knows all the words. And partly because our holiday decorations were still up.

Dad used to put the tree up one week before Christmas, and he always made sure it was down and the ornaments were neatly packed away before the new year. But ever since he married Sharon, he's become a lot more relaxed. Now we put the tree up the day after Thanksgiving and I love it!

Dad has always liked his life to be neat and

organized. His books are arranged alphabetically and his socks by color. Every morning Dad drinks precisely one and a half cups of coffee before heading off to work at his law firm.

Sharon, on the other hand, is pretty disorganized. She's been known to put the milk in the cupboard and the scissors in the refrigerator. Her style of housekeeping is relaxed at best. When she cooks, Sharon manages to dirty every pan in the kitchen. But you know the old saying — opposites attract. Dad and Sharon prove it. They're very happy together, and that makes me happy.

Before I tell you any more about my family, I should probably tell you about myself. I'm Mary Anne Spier. Age: thirteen. Height: average. (Okay, shorter than average.) Hair: brown and short. Eyes: brown. If you were to look for me at a school dance, you might not find me on the dance floor. The thought of dancing in front of people paralyzes me; I'm just too shy. You'd probably find me off to the side talking to my friends, or to my boyfriend, Logan.

I know it may be hard to imagine that someone so shy could have a boyfriend, but it's true. Logan Bruno and I have been in love — or at least, extreme like — practically since the day we met. Logan looks just like Cam Geary, the star (at least, *I* think so). He's got sparkling blue eyes, curly, brownish-blond hair, and a charming Kentucky accent.

For the past two days, Logan had been teasing me about our Christmas decorations. Because we put everything up so early, the wreath on the front door had turned almost completely brown, and the Christmas tree was drooping so much it looked as though the branches had lost the strength to hold up their ornaments. Which is why Logan was coming over — to help me take down the tree.

"Mary Anne!" Sharon called from the kitchen. "I found another one of Dawn's earrings."

"Give it to me, and I'll put it in the box with her nightgown, sweater, and barrette," I called back.

Dawn Schafer is my stepsister. She used to live with us, but she doesn't anymore. I really miss her.

You see, even before Dawn was my stepsister, she was one of my best friends. If we hadn't been friends, Dad and Sharon might never have gotten back together. (Notice I said *back* together?)

Shortly after we first met, Dawn and I were looking through our parents' old high school yearbooks. That's when we discovered that my dad and her mom used to date. And not just casually. They were in love, big time. But Sharon's parents didn't think Dad would amount to much (boy, were they surprised when he became a lawyer!), and they made Sharon stop seeing him. So Dad and Sharon went their separate ways, and married other people.

Dad and Mom were very happy together, but sadly, she died when I was just a baby. My grandmother, Verna Baker, tells me that I look and act just the way my mother did when she was my age. I can tell I remind Dad of my mother, too, because he sometimes gets this sad, misty expression when he's looking at me.

For the longest time it was just Dad and me, living together in a little house on Bradford Court. I told you he was organized and a major neatnik, but I didn't mention that there was a time when he was very strict. *Overprotective* is another way to put it.

I used to have to dress in really babyish clothes. I could only wear my hair in braids, and I was never allowed to talk on the phone for more then a few minutes at a time. I know he was doing what he thought he had to do as a single parent. But boy am I glad that's changed.

All this time Dawn was growing up with her family in California. After Dawn's mom

4

and dad divorced, Sharon brought Dawn and Dawn's younger brother Jeff back here to Stoneybrook. Jeff had trouble adjusting and returned to his dad quickly. Dawn loved her friends in Connecticut, but hated the cold winters, and she missed her family and friends in California, too. She finally decided she'd be happier living with her dad (and his new wife, Carol) in California.

Dawn writes me constantly, and we talk on the phone a lot. She even spent a few days with us at Christmas, and we had a blast. I think that's another reason I wanted to keep the Christmas decorations up. They reminded me of the fun Dawn and I had over the holidays.

When I talked to Dawn on New Year's Eve, she told me she was celebrating with Sunny Winslow, her best friend in California.

I spent New Year's Eve with Kristy Thomas, my best friend in Connecticut. We've known each other since we were in diapers. I can only remember a few New Year's Eves we didn't spend together. That night we were doing one of the things we love — baby-sitting. We watched Kristy's stepbrother and stepsister, Andrew and Karen, and her adopted sister, Emily Michelle. But I'll tell you more about them later.

Kristy had said she might come over today

to help Logan and me with the decorations. Kristy likes to keep busy and was getting anxious for school to start again. So was I.

"In the meadow we can build a snowman."

Sharon had switched to a new song. I wondered if she'd still be singing Christmas carols in February.

I gently shooed Tigger off my lap and moved to the kitchen door. "I'm going to put away the decorations today," I announced.

"So soon?" Sharon opened the dish towel drawer and deposited a frying pan inside.

I waited until Sharon turned back to the sink and then moved the frying pan to the cupboard. (There's a lot of my father in me.) "I wish we could keep them up forever," I said, "but if we wait any longer, I'm afraid this house will be declared a fire hazard."

"We don't want that," Sharon replied, drying her hands on a potholder. "This place pushes the limits as it is."

Sharon was referring to the fact that our farmhouse is two hundred years old and, naturally, is mostly wood.

When Dad married Sharon, he and I moved in here with Sharon and Dawn, because this house was much bigger than our old house on Bradford Court. Practically before we'd unpacked our suitcases, Dad decided we needed more smoke alarms. Now we have one in every room.

"Do you know where the storage box is?" I asked, helping Sharon put away the dishes.

"I'm sure it's in the attic." Sharon passed me several cereal bowls. "I think it's marked Table Linens."

That didn't surprise me one bit. Sharon has her own filing method, which has nothing to do with traditional logic.

"There used to be a red tablecloth inside," she explained. "But I lost that years ago." She paused for a moment. "It may still be in California. But the box is here."

"In the attic?" I asked with a gulp. The attic is not exactly my favorite place. It's dark and musty, and jammed full of old furniture and boxes. With the cobwebs and creaky floorboards, it is very easy to imagine a ghost living up there. (Yikes!)

Speaking of ghosts, Dawn swears this house has one. But not in the attic; in the secret passage. (I'm serious.) We actually have a passage that leads from Dawn's room to the barn. We think it may have been used to help slaves escape to freedom along the Underground Railroad.

"I think I'll wait until Logan is here to find the box." It's not that I think a boy would be less scared than me. It's just nice to have someone hold your hand when you walk up that dark flight of stairs searching for the light switch.

"And speaking of boxes," I added, "do you want me to mail Dawn's package? Logan and I could bring it to the post office this afternoon."

"That would be terrific." Sharon gestured toward a plate piled high with cookies on the kitchen table. "I just finished a fresh batch of honey granola snaps. I thought I'd slip in a dozen or so, since they're one of Dawn's favorites."

Notice Sharon didn't mention that they were one of *my* favorites? That's because they're not. Sharon and Dawn are practically vegetarians, and they eat a lot of healthy dishes made with tofu (ew) and seaweed (ick).

Dad and I prefer plain, simple steak and potatoes. And when it comes to cookies, I love good old-fashioned chocolate chip.

Ding-dong!

"That must be Logan," I exclaimed. "But what's he doing here so early? He wasn't supposed to come until noon."

Sharon tapped the clock on the microwave. "It's twelve o'clock on the dot!"

Where had the time gone? I had planned to spend the morning getting my clothes ready for school and cleaning my room. Instead, I'd been sitting in front of the fireplace, daydreaming.

Kristy and I had made lists of resolutions on New Year's Eve. But I brought mine home that night and promptly lost it. (Sometimes I think Sharon's absentmindedness is contagious!) It wasn't until two days later that I found it, under the throw pillows on our couch.

Here's what I wrote:

1. Do better in English
2. Write more letters to Dawn, make fewer calls.
3. Try to be a little more outgoing.

It was item three on the list that caused me to daydream for so long. Ever since Dawn left, I've really depended on my other best friend, Kristy. She's confident and outgoing and not afraid of anything. I've often wished that I could be more like her.

I wasn't aiming for a big change in my personality, I just wanted to be a little more confident about meeting new people. There are quite a few kids at school whom I like, but would like to know better.

Ding-dong.

"Oh, no!" I raced for the door. I was daydreaming again, and poor Logan was probably freezing on my front porch.

When I opened the door, Kristy was standing next to Logan. She was dressed in her trademark sweatshirt and jeans. Her straight brown hair was pulled back in a ponytail, which poked out the back of her baseball cap.

They both looked a little embarrassed.

"Have you got a broom handy?" Kristy asked.

"What for?" I asked.

Logan grinned sheepishly. "Kristy and I decided to take your wreath off the front door."

He held up a ring of bare twigs. Then Kristy pointed to a pile of brown needles by her feet and winced. "The whole thing just fell apart."

They both looked so mortified that I burst out laughing.

I think the three of us giggled our way through the rest of the afternoon. Every time we tried to get serious, something silly would happen.

For example, when Logan found the decorations box in the attic. It wasn't labeled Table Linens, as Sharon thought. It was marked Car Repair Kit.

Or when Kristy reached to remove an ornament from a branch of the tree and accidentally broke off the entire limb.

Tigger added to the hilarity, chasing an ornament into one of the Christmas stockings and getting tangled up inside.

10

In between giggles, we devoured Sharon's granola cookies (they're not bad when you're hungry) and talked about returning to school. All and all it was a fun day, the perfect end to our Christmas vacation.

CHAPTER 2

"Thirty-three right. Twenty-one left. Thirty-six right."

I tugged on my combination lock but it didn't open.

"What?" I checked the number above my head just to make sure I hadn't gone to the wrong locker. One thirty-two. That was my locker, all right. But why wouldn't it open?

Stoneybrook Middle School (SMS) can be a real zoo. Especially after a break. Today it seemed as if there were twice the usual number of students in the hall, and they were all talking at the tops of their lungs. Maybe that's why I was so confused.

There I stood, with one hand on my lock, and the other trying to balance my notebook, new pencil case, science book, math book, and gym suit. Kids were racing past me to their homerooms, and the clock was ticking.

If there's one thing I hate, it's being late for class. Everyone stares at you, including the teacher. Of course my face turns beet red and I feel like crying or throwing up or both.

"Thirty-*six* right, twenty-one left, and thirty-*three* right."

Tug. Nothing again. How could I have forgotten my locker combination? We'd only been out of school for two weeks. It wasn't as if it were two years.

"Having a problem?" a voice asked as my books slowly slid out of my arms and hit the floor.

I didn't even need to look. I recognized the voice. It was Alan Gray, one of my least favorite people at SMS. Alan thinks he's the class clown. I think he's the class pain. He never misses an opportunity to point out that you have a glob of ketchup on your blouse, or that your hair is messed up, or that you did something stupid when you thought no one was looking. I decided I'd try being honest with him. Maybe it would confuse him, and he'd leave me alone.

"I can't remember my locker combination," I confessed, turning back to try it once more before the bell rang.

Just to make me more tense, Alan peered over my shoulder. "You'd better hurry or you're going to be late."

"Gee, Alan," I muttered. "I wasn't aware of that."

Alan continued to breathe down my neck as he watched me carefully turn the dial. "Thirty-three. Twenty-one. Thirty-six."

"Aha!"he bellowed, nearly breaking my eardrum. "You forgot to turn it twice to the left."

I stared down at the lock. Alan was right. I had forgotten. I tried it once more and *voilà*! It opened. "Thanks for the help, Alan," I said, very sincerely. "I needed it."

Alan actually blushed. "Uh, no problem."

It was then that I realized the halls were almost empty, which meant I probably had less than a minute to shove my books in the locker, grab my English book, and race all the way to room 216.

"Hurry! Hurry!" Alan goaded as he jogged alongside me. "You're not going to make it, you're not going to make — !"

Brrrrring!

The bell drowned out the rest of his words and my entrance into class. I made a beeline for my desk and slid into my chair just as the bell finished ringing.

Mr. Blake, my homeroom teacher, called roll while I tried to get my heart back to its normal pulse rate. Finally I felt calm enough to look around the room. It was amazing. My class

14

looked as if it had just stepped out of a fashion magazine.

Everyone was wearing something new: flashy gold earrings, cool new jean jackets, bright white sneakers, wool sweaters and skirts. I was wearing the Christmas present my friend Claudia Kishi (whom I'll tell you about later) had given me. I'm usually a pretty conservative dresser, but this was a vest Claud had found at a vintage clothing store. She'd decorated it with funky pins and a burgundy silk rose corsage. I loved it.

I was wearing the vest, along with my denim skirt and a white blouse Dad had given me for Christmas.

When Mr. Blake finished calling roll, he moved to the first row of seats. "All right, everyone has thirty seconds to tell us about their entire Christmas vacation. I'll start."

He took a very deep breath and told his entire story without taking another breath of air.

"I took my family to Vermont to go skiing, we'd been looking forward to it all year; I had a brand-new pair of skis, a new ski sweater and gloves, we'd rented a condo for a whole week; I couldn't wait to hit the slopes but before I could even put my skis on, I tripped and sprained my ankle, and spent the entire vacation on crutches in the lodge."

Mr. Blake turned to Bruce Schermerhorn. "Your turn."

Bruce hadn't sprained his ankle but his family did miss their plane to their grandmother's and very nearly missed Christmas.

Here's what I said in my thirty seconds: "Dawn came for a visit and we decorated everything in the house, even the barn. We took cookies to some of our favorite baby-sitting charges and on Christmas Day we built a bunch of snowmen and dressed them in our old Halloween costumes. Then we roasted marshmallows in the fireplace and Sharon made a vegetarian meatloaf (ew!) and Dad cooked some steaks (yum), then Dawn went back to California and I miss her."

My voice was getting pretty squeaky by the end of my story, which made me blush (of course!) and the kids laugh. But I didn't mind that much because everyone sounded funny.

Homeroom whizzed by, and before I knew it I was taking a nice leisurely walk to my English class. It was fun seeing kids I hadn't seen all vacation, but my conversations started to sound a little like a broken record.

"Hi, Bea," I called when I passed Bea Foster. "How was your vacation?"

"Great. How was yours?"

I waved to Josh Freeman, a sixth grader who is the younger brother of my friend Amelia. "Hi, Josh, how was your vacation?"

"Great," Josh replied. "How was yours?"

After I had pretty much the same exchange with Amanda Martin, Bill Torrance, and Dorianne Wallingford, I almost wished someone would answer, "Terrible. Was yours as rotten as mine?" just for a little variety. But I guess everyone was happy to have had a vacation.

" 'All the world's a stage,' " Mrs. Simon, my English teacher, announced after the bell had rung. " 'And all the men and women merely players.' Can anyone tell me who wrote that?"

Several kids raised their hands.

"Yes, Amelia." Mrs. Simon nodded to the auburn-haired girl sitting next to me.

"Shakespeare," Amelia said in her soft voice. "And I think it's from the play *As You Like It*."

Mrs. Simon grinned. "Very good, Amelia. Right on both counts."

Amelia glanced sideways at me and I gave her my best "Way to go!" smile. She smiled back as her face turned bright red. Besides being one of the nicest girls at SMS, Amelia is also right up there with the smartest. But she isn't stuck up about it. In fact, she always seems to be a bit surprised when she answers questions correctly (which she does most of the time).

"William Shakespeare." Mrs. Simon pointed to a picture of a man with longish hair and a short, pointed beard wearing a white ruffled collar and black doublet. "This man, possibly the greatest writer of all time, was born in 1564 in Stratford-upon-Avon, England. Pencils were being manufactured for the first time. The only Europeans in North America lived in a Spanish settlement in St. Augustine, Florida. Shakespeare wrote thirty-seven plays during his lifetime. No other writer has been quoted more often, or had a greater influence on the cultural history of the western world than the bard of Stratford-upon-Avon."

Mrs. Simon's voice usually takes on a far-away, dreamy quality when she's talking about poetry or a writer she really loves. But this was the dreamiest, farthest-away sound I'd ever heard.

"Class, it will be my great pleasure this semester to introduce all of you to Mr. Shakespeare. Besides reading his words, we're going to find out about the man and the tumultuous times in which he lived."

Mrs. Simon gestured to the pictures and prints covering the walls of the classroom. There were bright posters from the Royal

Shakespeare Company in England, prints of paintings of men in short pointed beards, funny balloon pants, tights, and big buckled shoes, as well as beautiful color photos of romantic-looking castles.

Amelia leaned across the aisle and whispered, "Mrs. Simon must have come back to school a whole week early to do all of this decorating."

"She probably never left," I whispered back.

Picking up a piece of yellow chalk, Mrs. Simon wrote some words on the blackboard in big bold letters. Then she turned and announced, "I'm calling this project Meet Mr. Bill."

"Project?" Peter Hayes groaned from the back of the class. "We're going to have to do a project?"

Personally, I like projects. They're more fun than sitting and listening to a lecture. But Peter Hayes is the type who can make a teacher's (especially a substitute teacher's) life miserable.

"Don't worry, Peter," Mrs. Simon said patiently, "you won't be by yourself. I've divided the class into groups of four. Each group will be in charge of making a presentation to the class."

Mrs. Simon then picked up a basket and walked down the aisle, distributing buttons.

19

"Will Power," Barbara Hirsch said, reading her button out loud.

Brian Hall's button had a picture of Shakespeare in a cowboy hat, and the words, "Howdy, Bard!" Everyone laughed at that one.

Another button showed Shakespeare sporting a baseball cap and holding a bat. It read, "Play Bill!" Most of the guys wanted that button.

Amelia and I were both happy to receive Will Power buttons. As I pinned mine to my vest, Mrs. Simon announced the groups. I couldn't believe my luck — Mrs. Simon had put me in the same study group as Amelia, Gordon Brown, and Barbara Hirsch.

I really like Gordon. He was in my Modern Living class, and he was a good sport about having to pretend-marry Howie Johnson when there weren't enough girls to go around. And Barbara Hirsch, besides being really nice, has been Amelia's best friend since second grade. I couldn't help smiling. We were going to have fun!

"I've made a list of some suggestions for projects," Mrs. Simon said, handing out sheets of paper. "But you kids are welcome to put your heads together and come up with your own ideas. Just remember, we want to know more about William Shakespeare, the world he lived in, and the people he might have known."

Amelia, Gordon, Barbara and I pulled our desks together and started brainstorming.

The list was actually a lot of questions. As I read each one out loud, the others in my group either winced or smiled. Barbara was probably the most outspoken. She gave a firm thumbs-up or thumbs-down to each question.

"Who was England's sovereign, and what influence did he or she have on William Shakespeare's work?" got a thumbs-down from Barbara. "Who might have been Shakespeare's friends?" got a thumbs-up.

"I really like number three," Gordon said, pointing to the question and reading it out loud. " 'What was happening in Shakespeare's world?' I have a big timeline chart at home on the wall of my room. We could use it to work on this question."

"Great," Amelia said. "My brother Josh has a book called *Timetables of History*. I'm sure there's some good information in there, too."

I had already taken a piece of notebook paper out of my notebook and written *Meet Mr. Bill* at the top. Underneath I'd neatly printed the names of the people in my group. I checked the clock. We had about ten more minutes to plan. We were going to need more time.

"Why don't we meet after school tomorrow and talk about this?" I suggested. "We could go to my house."

"Okay," Amelia said. "I'll bring Josh's book and Gordon can bring his timeline — "

"And I'll bring the snacks," Barbara chimed in. "We can't think on an empty stomach."

"Just so long as the snacks have chocolate chips in them," Gordon kidded. "My brain really responds well to chocolate."

"I'll make some lemonade," I added. "And tea."

Amelia cocked her head. "This is starting to sound more like a party than a study session."

"It's a study party," Barbara said. "Where the best minds will come up with the best ideas."

I could feel myself grinning. With a great group like this, how could we lose?

CHAPTER 3

"This meeting of the Baby-sitters Club is officially called to order," Kristy Thomas announced in her most presidential way. She tugged on her green visor (which she often wears during meetings) and leaned forward in Claudia's director's chair (where she always sits). "My first order of business is to wish everyone a Happy New Year."

"Happy New Year!" we shouted back.

Who are we? Only the most amazing group of baby-sitters ever to assemble in one room. Seriously, we are the BSC.

The idea for the club was Kristy's (of course). Kristy has a zillion ideas a day, and most of them are great. This particular idea hit her one afternoon while she was listening to her mom make call after call to find a sitter for her younger brother, David Michael. Wouldn't it be great, Kristy thought, if Mom could make one phone call and reach several baby-sitters?

Before you could say the words, "Let's form a club," Kristy had done just that.

In the beginning, there were only four of us — Kristy, me, Claudia Kishi, and Stacey McGill. But we soon had more clients then we knew what to do with, so we opened the club to more members. Now there are seven of us, plus two associate members (who fill in when none of the regular members can take a job).

We run the BSC like a business because that's what it is. Three times a week — on Mondays, Wednesdays, and Fridays — we meet from five-thirty to six o'clock. Kristy's really strict about the time, too. When the numbers on Claudia's digital clock turn from 5:29 to 5:30, that's it, the meeting begins. If you're even one minute late, Kristy is not happy.

Our meetings are held in Claudia's room, because she is the only one of us with her own phone line.

During that half hour, clients call, I check our schedules, and one of us agrees to take the job.

Kristy is our president, of course. But not just because she founded the club. Kristy is a real leader. She's energetic and outspoken. I love her dearly, but I have to say that some-

24

times she can be bossy. She's also a super athlete and the coach of Kristy's Krushers, a softball team for little kids who don't play in Little League.

Kristy's always organizing something, whether it's a backyard circus with our charges, or some fun activity for her family. And believe me, an activity with her family is a major event.

Here's who she lives with: her mom; her stepfather, Watson; her two older brothers, Charlie and Sam; and her younger brother, David Michael. Wait, I'm not finished. There's also her adopted sister, two-year-old Emily Michelle, and her grandmother, Nannie. Plus every other month, Karen and Andrew, Watson's kids from his first marriage, live with them, too. Those are just the people (ten all together). Now add the pets: one very grumpy cat named Boo-Boo, a Bernese mountain dog puppy named Shannon, a hermit crab, one rat, and two goldfish. That's an awful lot of pets and people under one roof!

Luckily, Kristy lives in a mansion. Why? Because Watson Brewer is a genuine millionaire. (Cool, huh?)

Even with all of her activities at home and school, Kristy is always thinking of new ways to improve our club. She was the one who dreamed up Kid-Kits.

What are Kid-Kits? They're large boxes that we decorated with sequins, glitter glue, Magic Markers, and paints. Each one is filled with coloring books, old toys, stickers, and anything else we think might be fun for our charges to play with. Kids love them. They're terrific ice-breakers. And on a rainy day I wouldn't be caught without mine.

Kristy also started the club notebook, in which each of us writes up every sitting job. Then we read each other's entries. That way, we stay up to date on what's happening with our clients.

While Kristy is our president and idea person, Claudia Kishi is the BSC's vice-president and resident artist. She tie-dyes shirts, creates papier-mâché animal earrings and pins, and makes cool collages out of things she just picks up on the street.

Even her outfits are works of art. Today she was wearing a black derby hat with a red-and-white polka dot ribbon, which matched her "ruby slippers" (high-top sneakers with red sequins). Black-and-white striped trousers with red suspenders, and a black long-sleeved T-shirt completed the outfit.

Claudia is a knock-out. She's Asian-American, with long silky black hair and a perfect, I mean, *perfect* (not a zit in sight) complexion. I find this pretty amazing, since Claudia has a real thing for junk food. Cheez doodles, Malomars, candy kisses, pretzels — you name it, Claud probably has it stashed somewhere in her room. (She hides it because she's not supposed to eat junk food, especially so close to dinner time.) Her favorite not-so-secret hiding place is inside a fake book.

Claudia is outgoing and fun to be with, but her life isn't exactly perfect. You see, she's a very smart person, but a terrible student. School is a major struggle for her. What makes this doubly hard is that she has an older sister who is a real live genius. Janine Kishi is already taking college classes and she's still in high school. We're talking major brain.

Now Stacey McGill, Claudia's best friend, is the opposite of Claudia when it comes to school. She's a good student, especially in math, which is why we voted her treasurer of the club. Of all of us, Stacey is probably the most sophisticated and stylish. I think this is because she grew up in New York City. That may sound glamorous, but Stacey's life has definitely not been.

You see, Stacey has diabetes, a disease that interferes with the way her body processes sugar. That means she has to watch what she eats. Always. Not only that, she has to give herself insulin injections every single day (ew!). And if dealing with a life-long illness

27

wasn't hard enough, Stacey also had to go through her parents' divorce. That was a rough time, but with a little help from all of us Stacey was able to handle it.

Then, not long ago, Stacey felt she'd outgrown her friends in the BSC. When she started dating Robert Brewster, Stacey thought that his friends were more sophisticated then hers. She made a choice to hang out with Robert's friends. We (the club members) had a major falling out with Stacey, and she left the BSC. Then she realized that, although the other crowd may have been ultra-cool and trendy, when the chips were down and she really needed a friend, they weren't there for her.

Stacey asked to return to the club and was accepted. I'm so glad. I really missed her.

As treasurer, Stacey collects our dues, which we use to pay Claudia's phone bill, and Kristy's brother Charlie to chauffeur her and our newest member, Abby Stevenson, to and from meetings. (No, he doesn't drive a limousine. Charlie's car is an old beat-up green thing appropriately named the Junk Bucket.)

Now on to the club secretary. Did you guess it was me? I was chosen because I have the neatest handwriting, and because I'm organized (like Dad). It's my job to keep the club record book. Not only do I make sure all of our clients' addresses and phone numbers are up to date, but I keep track of their children's allergies, birthdays, favorite foods, toys, etc.

I also write down every member's personal schedule, which can be pretty complicated, since I have to think about Kristy's Krushers practices, Claudia's art classes, Stacey's doctor appointments, and so on. When a client calls, I can tell at a glance which one of us is free to take the job. I'm proud to say that I have never, ever made a mistake. (Knock on wood!)

That brings me to our alternate officer and newest member, Abigail Stevenson. Abby recently moved to Stoneybrook, from Long Island. You'd think, as a new kid, she might have been a little nervous about starting at SMS. Not Abby. She just jumped right in. She says whatever comes into her head. (Usually it's something funny.) Abby has long dark curly hair, wears glasses or contacts (depending on her mood), has asthma, and is allergic to practically everything. But Abby's far from sickly. In fact she's a terrific athlete (she swears she was born in soccer shorts). I would say that Abby was truly one of a kind, except for one thing — she's an identical twin!

You know how some twins walk, talk, and dress exactly alike? Well, not the Stevensons. Abby's sister, Anna, looks exactly like her, but that's where the similarity ends. Anna wears her hair short, she has no allergies or asthma, and couldn't care less about sports. Music is her first love. Anna is an excellent violinist. She's already landed a spot in the SMS orchestra. She's friendly and confident, but not outspoken like Abby. It's funny that two people who look so much alike could be so different.

Abby's mom is what Abby calls a workaholic. Ever since the death of Abby's father, Mrs. Stevenson has thrown herself into her job. She commutes into New York City and works long hours, which means Abby and Anna spend a lot of time on their own. It's a good thing they have each other, or they could get pretty lonely. I know I would.

Fortunately, they also live only two doors down from Kristy's huge family, and right across the street from Shannon Kilbourne, another BSC member.

Shannon, who has thick, curly blonde hair and high cheekbones, goes to a private school called Stoneybrook Day. She's always busy with extracurricular activities there, but somehow she manages to find time for the BSC.

In the past, Shannon has filled in as a full-time member, when Dawn went on an extended visit to California, and while Stacey was gone. Now Shannon is an associate member again. Logan, my boyfriend, is our other associate. As I mentioned before, we call on them when we are swamped and need an extra sitter, but they don't have to attend the regular meetings.

Everyone in the club is thirteen and in the eighth grade, except for our junior officers, Mallory Pike and Jessica Ramsey. Mal and Jessi are best friends. They are eleven years old and in the sixth grade. Both have pierced ears, and both adore horses — and any movie, book, or video game that has a horse in it. I don't know how many times they've read Marguerite Henry's *Misty of Chincoteague*, but I do know they've seen *The Black Stallion* at least twenty times. They recite the lines along with the actors. (I *don't* recommend watching it with them.)

I've told you how they're alike. Here's how they're different: First, in terms of appearance. Jessi is black and Mallory is white. Jessi is tall and thin, with beautiful brown eyes and long legs. Mallory has auburn hair, wears glasses and braces (which she hates), and is medium height. Second, in terms of interests. Jessi plans to go to New York and be a famous ballerina one day. (I know she will — Jessi's very talented.) Mallory plans to be a children's book author and illustrator. Last, in terms of family. Jessi has one sister, Becca, who's eight, and a two-year-old brother, John Philip, Junior (alias Squirt). Mallory has seven — count them, *seven* — brothers and sisters, all under the age of eleven. First come the triplets: Adam, Jordan, and Byron (ten years old), then Vanessa (nine), Nicky (eight), Margo (seven), and finally Claire (five).

Mal and Jessi do a lot of afternoon baby-sitting and can only baby-sit at night for their own siblings.

I think that covers everyone. Now back to our New Year's celebration.

"This calls for a snack." Claudia held up a bag of pretzels (for Stacey) and a plate piled high with cookies that she had made herself. They were shaped like top hats, with the words Happy New Yeer! written on them. (Spelling isn't one of Claud's strong points.)

Abby snatched one of the cookies and said, "If this isn't going to be the best new year ever, I'll eat my hat." Then she bit into her cookie and burst out laughing, which made her spew crumbs all over Mal and Jessi.

"Ew!" Mallory and Jessi hopped up, swiping at their hair and shoulders. Now the crumbs were all over the rug. Claud pointed to the floor and said, "Pick that up, or I'll make you eat *my* hat!" At which point we all burst into giggles.

Usually Kristy frowns on too much silliness during our meetings, but she just grinned at me and held out her hand. "Pass the hat, will you?"

If there was a record for fastest consumption of a plate of cookies, I think we would have broken it that afternoon. But in the midst of all of that munching, we still managed to schedule four sitting jobs. Just before the meeting ended, Claudia passed around glasses of apple cider.

Stacey raised her cup. "I'd like to propose a toast to Dawn, whose body is in California with the We Love Kids Club, but whose spirit remains here with the BSC in Connecticut."

I raised my cup, my eyes starting to brim with tears. (I forgot to mention, I'll cry at anything.) "To Dawn."

Kristy raised her cup and smiled at me. "And to the Baby-sitters Club: the best friends a girl could have."

That did it. I cried.

CHAPTER 4

On Thursday the halls at SMS were rowdier than ever. Every time I stepped out of class I wanted to cover my ears.

Sometime after English, and before Social Studies, someone slipped me a note in the hall. I didn't even see who it was. I just felt someone touch my arm and a piece of paper was tucked into my hand. Things were so hectic I didn't remember to read it until last period. Here's what it said:

Mary Anne,
  Gordon just whispered "William Tells All" to me. He said Barbara whispered it to him. What do you think of it as a title of our project? I think it's cool. Meet you after school — front steps. B there or B □.
                                A.F.

I couldn't help smiling. Amelia and others were already hard at work on our English project. This was going to be fun.

After the final bell rang, Claudia and Stacey met me at my locker. Claudia was carrying a huge cardboard carton.

"Are you on trash patrol today?" I asked as I eyed the rusty tin can, twisted coat hanger, and green rubber boots with funny buckles inside the box.

"Trash?" Claudia gasped in mock horror. "Bite your tongue. These treasures are going to be part of my new invention."

"Invention?" Stacey repeated. "Since when did you become Mr. Science?"

"That's Ms. Art to you," Claudia said. "And my class assignment is to create a Rube Goldberg invention."

Stacey and I gave Claudia our blankest stares.

"Hello?" Claud snapped her fingers in front of our faces. "Anybody home? You're supposed to ask me who Rube Goldberg was."

Stacey and I exchanged glances and shrugged. We asked in unison, "Who was Rube Goldberg?"

"He was a cartoonist who made wacky inventions," Claud replied. "Rube Goldberg created those funny contraptions. For instance, a Ping-Pong ball rolls down a tube, runs into a domino that falls against a button that starts a water wheel that knocks over a few other things, then runs into an army boot that kicks a bucket. All of this to turn on a lamp or something."

Stacey and I looked at each other again, trying hard not to laugh. "Oh, *that* Rube Goldberg," I said.

Of course we burst into giggles, which made Claudia huffy. "Well, for your information, he was very famous, and sculptures of his inventions are at museums around the world and are worth millions."

"I believe you," I said, struggling to keep a straight face. "It's just that the idea of an old army boot kicking a bucket being famous and worth lots of money makes me laugh."

Claudia thought about it for a second. Then a smile crept across her lips. "You're right, it is funny. In fact, it's ridiculous. That's why I love it."

Gordon Brown popped his head into our group. "I hope you're not discussing our English project, because words like ridiculous make me nervous."

"Don't worry, Gordon." I gestured toward the box Claudia held in her arms. "We were discussing art."

"Oh." Gordon nodded. "That makes sense, then."

On the front steps we met Amelia, who patted a package wrapped in green plastic under her arm. "I had to promise Josh on a stack of Bibles that I wouldn't lose his *Timetables of History* book. He made me put it inside this plastic trash bag, just in case we had a blizzard or freak thunderstorm."

Gordon gestured with his thumb over his shoulder. "My chart's in my backpack."

"The chocolate-filled brain food is in here," Barbara said, holding up a plastic lunch pail decorated with Casper the Ghost.

I pointed toward the direction of my house. "Onward and upward."

Stacey and Claudia walked part of the way with us, planning the most outrageous Rube Goldberg invention of all, using kids' discarded toys and food.

Once inside my house, Barbara broke out the cookies. I made some tea and poured everyone lemonade, and then we settled down to work.

It was amazing how well we worked together.

"Barbara thought up the title, *William Tells All*," Gordon said as he unfolded his timeline on the carpet in front of the fireplace. "I think it's perfect."

Amelia took a bite of cookie and nodded. "Sounds very cool."

"We could do a timeline of events that happened when Shakespeare lived," I suggested. "Or we could put together a scrapbook, or — " I didn't realize that while I was talking, I had been looking around the room. My eyes fell on yesterday's edition of the *Stoneybrook News*. "Or we could make a newspaper."

"Ummpph!" Amelia spit cookies everywhere (the second crumb spray in two days). "Great idea, Mary Anne!"

I told you that Kristy is usually the great idea person, so I was particularly happy to hear Amelia say that.

Barbara waved her hands excitedly. "If it's called *William Tells All* we could have a gossip column about who's dating who, and we could have a theatre review of one of his plays."

"Yes!" Gordon pumped one fist in the air. "And we could have news from the foreign correspondent, with the latest update on Sir Francis Drake's voyage around the world."

"And we could have a police report," I added, "and list who Queen Elizabeth arrested, and who she put in the tower, like Mary Queen of Scots."

"And a poet's corner!" Barbara cried. "We could print one of Shakespeare's sonnets and maybe one of Edmund Spenser's poems."

"And we could even do an Elizabethan *Hints from Heloise*," Amelia exclaimed. "With advice on how to repair a thatched roof, or what to do if you get a run in your tights."

Everyone was so excited that we were literally shouting our ideas at each other, but I didn't mind at all. In fact, I loved it.

"We'll have a Dear Ann Landers–type column," Gordon said.

"And horoscopes," Barbara added.

"We could even write the classifieds, selling old wagons and harpsichords." I was so excited my voice squeaked, which made everyone laugh.

"This is going to be so much fun," Amelia said, when she'd stopped giggling. "I wish we didn't have to go to any other classes."

"Me, too," I said, thinking about math class in particular.

"We better write these brilliant ideas down now," Barbara said, "before we forget."

I grabbed my pen and yellow pad. "Ready."

"Why don't we look at the timeline," Gordon said, gesturing toward his chart, "and write next to each category what events happened, and in what year."

Amelia wiped her hands on her napkin and reached for Josh's book. "I'll check the timetables."

Barbara uncapped her pen. "Why don't I keep track of who wants to write what articles?"

We worked intensely for the next hour or so. We probably would have gone on longer if Amelia hadn't had to leave.

"Sorry, you guys," she said, carefully re-wrapping her brother's book in the plastic trash bag. "Mom and Dad are taking us out to this new Italian restaurant that's on the way to the mall. It's called Pietro's."

"Italian food?" Gordon suddenly looked as if he might be a little hungry.

Amelia grinned wickedly. "Spaghetti with meatballs, three-inch-thick lasagna, fettucini alfredo, cannelloni — "

"Stop!" Barbara ordered. "If you mention one more thing, you're going to have to take us all with you."

Amelia's eyes widened. "I wish you could come. That would be fun."

"Not me," I said, shaking my head. "It's my night to make dinner. I promised to make cheese enchiladas."

"Besides, we couldn't all fit in your dad's little car," Barbara pointed out.

We laughed. Amelia's father owned a tiny old Volkswagen Bug that he'd restored to mint condition. It was his pride and joy, but definitely not a crowd-carrier.

"It was just an idea," Amelia said with a good-natured shrug. "Anyway, I promise to give a full report tomorrow."

We agreed to have our next meeting over the weekend. As the group walked out my front door, Amelia turned around and smiled. "I'm really excited about this project. You guys are the best!"

After they left, I had that little butterfly feeling of excitement inside me. I felt good about the project, *and* good that I was being more outgoing and making new friends. I hadn't just sat quietly listening to everyone else's ideas; I'd tossed in several good ones of my own.

I flipped on the radio and danced around the kitchen while I prepared dinner. *Prepared* is kind of an exaggeration — the enchiladas were frozen, so all I had to do was put them in the oven and whip up a salad.

That night Dad and Sharon and I ate dinner in the dining room. I even set out placemats and lit the candles.

"What is this?" Dad asked, smiling at me in the glow of the candlelight. "Some sort of special occasion?"

I smiled back. "Nothing special," I replied. "I'm just happy about school, and — well, everything."

Dad reached across the table and patted my hand. "I'm happy you're happy."

Across the table Sharon was beaming and I took her hand, completing our circle.

After dinner, I went to my room and finished my homework. Then I snuggled under the covers of my bed with Tigger, whose motor was going full tilt. I put my pillow on my lap, pulled out a piece of pale yellow stationery from my bedside table, and started a letter to Dawn.

As I put pen to paper, I heard the distant wail of an ambulance siren, on the other side of town. Sirens always sound eerie at night, and a twinge of apprehension made me shiver. I shook my head to get rid of the unpleasant feeling, then turned my attention back to Dawn's letter.

I couldn't wait to tell her about my English project, Claudia's art project, and the great time I'd had with Gordon, Barbara, and Amelia.

CHAPTER 5

B*eep-beep. Beep-beep. Beep-beep.*

In my dream, a car was beeping at me underwater. Then the images swirled and it became the timer on the oven. Had I forgotten the enchiladas? Finally the images swirled once more and I surfaced.

It was my alarm clock. It had been beeping for nearly a half hour.

I tossed back the covers and leaped out of bed. "Why didn't someone tell me?"

If Dawn had still been living with us, she would have yelled from my doorway, "Rise and shine, sleepyhead."

But Dawn was in California. And I was in Stoneybrook, about to be late for school. Where was Dad? Usually he would flip my light switch up and down in that irritating way. But not today.

"Sharon? Have you seen my navy blue socks?" I heard Dad call from the hall. Then he ran past the door of my room in his navy blue suit and bare feet, and pounded down the stairs, which is not his usual style.

Dad must have overslept, too.

I ran into the bathroom, hopped in the shower, and squealed as the first freezing cold drops hit my shoulders. Too many seconds later, the cold turned lukewarm. Old houses and their plumbing can make you nuts.

After the shortest shower on record, I raced back to my room, threw on the first things I could find — a jean skirt, red cotton sweater and loafers — then made a beeline for the stairs.

"In conclusion, I would like to say it has been a pleasure working on this project. The research I've done has only made me be more — no. After having done the research, I feel that I'm — no."

I stuck my head in the kitchen. Sharon was standing in front of the kitchen window in her burgundy suit and heels. She held a piece of toast in one hand and a glass of orange juice in the other and was smiling at her reflection.

She saw me and said, "My big presentation is this morning. Which do you like better: 'This product has a new fan in me'; or, 'After all the research I've done, I've become a big supporter of this product'?"

I wasn't really awake but I gave the best answer I could. "The short one is better," I replied, hurrying to the cupboard for a bowl and the box of cereal. "But I like what you said in the second one."

Sharon took a bite of her toast and chewed vigorously. "You're right." She turned back to face the window. "In conclusion, I'd like to say this product has my total support!"

"Much better." I poured the milk on my cereal, eyeing the clock. I had about two minutes to eat, brush my teeth, grab my homework, mail my letter to Dawn, and be on my way to school. Impossible!

I didn't even bother to sit down, I just picked up the bowl and spooned the cereal into my mouth as fast as I could.

"Mary Anne!" Sharon gasped, suddenly noticing what I was doing. "You're going to make yourself sick. Slow down."

"Can't!" I yelled, racing from the room. "Gotta run."

I managed to accomplish everything on my list and then bolted out the door, just in time to meet Mal and Stacey at the corner.

"Did you listen to the radio this morning?" Stacey asked.

"No," I said, trying to fluff my hair, which was still damp from the shower. "I overslept, and then Sharon was rehearsing her speech for a big presentation at work. What happened?''

"I guess there was a car accident outside of town last night," Stacey replied. "But I only caught the tail end of the report. I didn't hear any details."

Mallory pointed to Claudia, who was waiting for us at the next corner. "Maybe Claud heard. She always listens to the radio."

I grinned. "Yeah, in hopes that school will be canceled due to snow, or rain, or — "

"Or a heat wave," Logan added, running up beside me.

"How long have you been there?" I asked in surprise. "I didn't even hear you."

"That's because there's shampoo in your ear," Logan said, swiping at a patch of bubbles that had dried on my cheek.

I could feel myself blush down to the roots of my hair. "I was running late," I confessed. "I must not have rinsed completely."

Normally Logan would have cracked a joke at my response, but by that time we'd reached Claudia, and the look on her face stopped him.

"Did you hear?" she asked. "There was a terrible accident by the highway just outside of town. One person was killed. A thirteen-year-old from Stoneybrook."

We all gasped.

"Did they give the name?" I whispered, afraid to hear the answer.

Claudia shook her head. "They said they're waiting until the relatives have been notified."

"It might be someone from our school," Stacey said. "Or maybe from Stoneybrook Day."

Normally my friends and I laugh and joke while we walk to school. Not today. Just the thought that someone we knew might have died put a dark cloud over everything.

The main building of Stoneybrook Middle School loomed in the distance, and my heart started thudding faster. I think everyone's did.

Logan voiced what we all were thinking. "The teachers must know who it was. We'll probably find out this morning."

"The other kids may know right now," Stacey murmured. "I mean, look at the school-yard. Usually everyone's laughing and talking, and running around. But everything seems so still."

Stacey was right. It did look different. Kids stood together in tight little groups. Every so often someone would glance over her shoulder at the building. But there wasn't the usual joking chatter. There was barely any sound.

Jessi was the last to join us. She hurried to us with the same grim look on her face. "The

TV said there was a car accident across town last night, by the overpass, and someone was killed."

"A thirteen-year-old," Claudia repeated.

My heart rate suddenly jumped up a notch. Most of my closest friends were walking beside me, alive and well. But not my best friend, Kristy.

What if the dead student were Kristy? She lived across town and rode the bus to school. Maybe Charlie had been driving her somewhere in the Junk Bucket last night, and . . .

I held my breath for the last half block until we reached the school grounds. Standing next to Abby, wearing her standard uniform of jeans, turtleneck, and baseball cap, was Kristy. I was never so glad to see anyone in my life.

"Kristy!" I threw my arms around her and gave her a big hug. "I can't tell you how glad I am to see you."

"You, too," Kristy said, hugging me back hard. I knew in that second that she had been worrying, too.

Before we could say any more, Emily Bernstein, the editor of the *SMS Express*, entered the school grounds in tears and ran up the steps.

Kristy looked at me and murmured, "Emily knows who it is."

Even though the warning bell hadn't rung,

we followed Emily into the building. The halls were packed and I could only catch snatches of conversation.

"A drunk driver ran a stop sign and broadsided them," Pete Black, the eighth-grade class president, was saying to some friends.

"Who was hit?" Abby demanded.

"I don't know." Pete gestured to the school office, where the outlines of several people were visible through the frosted glass. "The teachers are meeting in Mr. Kingbridge's office right now. I'm sure they'll tell us soon."

Mallory and Jessi had gotten another report. "Benny Ott told me he heard it was a family of four in the car," Mallory said, "but only the daughter was killed."

"So it's a girl," Claudia said in a shaky voice. Outside the cafeteria, I could see several girls sobbing and hugging each other. I watched as Trevor Sandbourne put his arm around his girlfriend, who wept into his shoulder.

Part of me wanted to ask them to tell me what they knew. But another part of me didn't know if I could bear the news. Clearly, whoever had been killed had a lot of friends at SMS. Was I one of them?

Logan had left to put his books in his locker. When he returned, he said, "I found out that the car was a VW."

"Whose car?" Kristy asked. "The drunk's, or the student's?"

Logan frowned. "I'm not sure."

"A VW?" I was starting to get a cold tingly feeling on my arms and legs. There weren't very many students at our school whose family owned a Volkswagen. The pieces were starting to pile up. I just couldn't let myself put them together.

The first and second bells had rung, signaling that school had begun, but most of the students ignored them. I vaguely remembered that I was supposed to be in Mr. Blake's homeroom, but I just couldn't make myself leave my friends.

"May I have your attention, please." Mr. Kingbridge's voice came over the public address system. "There will be a special assembly this morning. Will all students and teachers please walk in a calm, orderly manner to the auditorium? Thank you."

Logan hooked his arm through mine. "This is it," he said softly. "Let's go hear the bad news."

We sat a few rows from the front of the stage. Logan was on one side of me; Kristy was on the other. Claudia, Stacey, and Abby sat next to Kristy. Mallory and Jessi were in the seats behind them.

Usually, when SMS students take their seats

for an assembly, the noise is deafening. Not today. It was eerily quiet. Behind us I could hear several girls weeping softly. Aside from the sharp noise of footsteps in the aisles, the only other sound was hushed whispering.

I felt as if I were in a church, not a middle school auditorium. The atmosphere reminded me of when Claudia's grandmother, Mimi, died, and we went to her funeral.

After a few agonizing minutes, Mr. Kingbridge, our assistant principal, and Mrs. Amer, one of the school's guidance counselors, walked onto the stage. Usually Mr. Kingbridge uses a microphone to address the school, but he didn't need one today. You could have heard a pin drop.

His shoulders were slumped and he looked tired and old.

"Students," Mr. Kingbridge began, "I have some very sad news. Last night, the Freeman family was in a terrible accident."

I clutched Kristy's hand so tightly my nails dug into her hand. "Oh, no," I whispered, squeezing my eyes closed.

"A drunk driver, going too fast, ran a stop sign and struck their car broadside," Mr. Kingbridge continued. "Mr. and Mrs. Freeman and Josh suffered some broken bones, but are expected to recover completely. The other driver also had minor injuries." He cleared his throat.

"However, I'm sad to say that Amelia was killed on impact."

Tears poured down my cheeks as I hugged Kristy, and then Logan. "It's not possible," I sobbed into Logan's shoulder. "I just saw her yesterday."

All the color had drained from Logan's face.

Now the auditorium really did sound like a funeral. Students were crying openly, and holding each other.

"Death is always a shock," Mr. Kingbridge continued. "But when it comes to someone so young and full of life, it's almost too much to bear. Amelia will be greatly missed and I know all of our hearts go out to the Freeman family." He dug in the pocket of his suit for a handkerchief, then wiped at his own eyes and blew his nose.

Mrs. Amer touched Mr. Kingbridge on the shoulder, then turned to face the assembly. "Classes will continue today, but anyone who feels the need to go home may do so if their parents come to school to pick them up. For those of you who wish to stay, but feel the need to talk to someone, I've arranged for grief counselors to be on call in the guidance office. This is a devastating time for all of us. Please don't be afraid to ask for help."

"Thank you, Mrs. Amer," Mr. Kingbridge said. "One last thing. Funeral services for

Amelia will be held on Monday at eleven A.M. at the First Methodist Church. Any student who wishes to attend will be excused from class."

Even after Mr. Kingbridge and Mrs. Amer left the stage, no one moved. The thought of going to class seemed absurd. But there really wasn't anything we could do except cry. For Amelia. For her family. And for ourselves.

We (practically every member of the Baby-sitters Club) sat in the auditorium for nearly an hour. Every few minutes one of us would break down and cry. It just didn't seem possible that something so awful could have happened to someone our age, someone we knew.

When I finally started to stand up, Kristy clutched my hand and whispered, "Please don't go. Not yet."

Somehow I understood exactly what Kristy was feeling. Being confronted with the fact that somebody could be alive one minute and gone the next made us want to hold on tightly to our friends and family.

I think the only class I attended that day was English, with Mrs. Simon.

Gordon Brown was sitting by my desk, waiting for me when I came into the classroom. "Is Barbara here?" I whispered, slipping into my seat.

Gordon's eyes were swollen and rimmed

with red. He shook his head sadly. "No, but I'm not surprised. Barbara is Amelia's best friend. . . . I guess I should say, was."

Mrs. Simon, who usually is so confident and together, was subdued and quiet. She spent the first few minutes of class walking around the room and talking to each of us individually. When she came to Gordon and me, she squeezed my hand and said to the class, "Why don't we pull our desks in a circle and talk about what has happened?"

My eyes immediately filled with tears.

"I can't believe some drunk just *killed* her, and he's still alive," Jeff Cummings grumbled from across the circle. He was usually pretty quiet but today he seemed angry. "It's just not fair."

"I think what's hardest to accept," I said, trying to keep my voice from breaking, "is that we'll never see Amelia again. Death is so, so final."

Mrs. Simon pursed her lips. I could see she was trying not to cry, too. "It does seem that way. But remember, Mary Anne, Amelia will live on in our memories."

That made me think of the last image I had of Amelia. The moment when she was leaving my house and paused to smile at me over her shoulder. Her cheeks were flushed pink from the excitement at our meeting and her grin seemed to stretch from ear to ear. Amelia was so full of joy and life. How could she be gone?

I walked the halls that day, seeing life in a new scary light. My world, which had seemed so solid and comfortable, felt as if it had been hit by an earthquake. My emotions flipped from sadness to fear to despair as I realized that, if someone as wonderful as Amelia could be taken from us this way, so could anyone. At any moment. And for no reason.

When the last bell had finally rung, and I'd said good-bye to Logan and Kristy and my other friends, I trudged home feeling like the oldest person on the planet.

CHAPTER 6

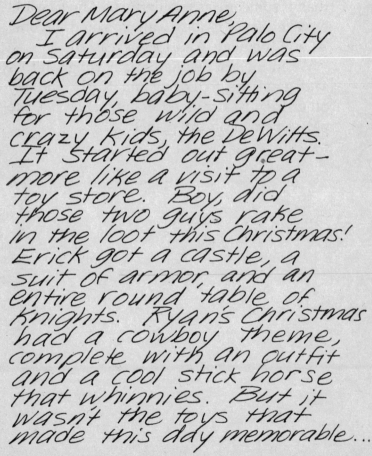

Dear Mary Anne,
   I arrived in Palo City on Saturday and was back on the job by Tuesday, baby-sitting for those wild and crazy kids, the DeWitts. It started out great— more like a visit to a toy store. Boy, did those two guys rake in the loot this Christmas! Erick got a castle, a suit of armor, and an entire round table of knights. Ryan's Christmas had a cowboy theme, complete with an outfit and a cool stick horse that whinnies. But it wasn't the toys that made this day memorable...

Going to the mailbox is usually one of my favorite things to do — it holds so much promise. There can be one of my magazines, a fun catalogue, an announcement that I've won the lottery, or best of all, a letter from a friend.

On Thursday afternoon, I stopped at the mailbox as usual, but I barely glanced at the letters and magazines inside. I felt depressed.

I needed to talk to someone in my family. Dad and Sharon weren't home, and because of the three-hour time difference, I had to wait until six to call Dawn. So I walked into the living room and sat on the couch, staring at the unlit fireplace.

Tigger padded down the stairs and hopped into my lap, knocking the mail onto the floor.

"Mousekins, you naughty boy," I murmured, scratching him between the ears (his favorite spot). "You've been sleeping on my pillow upstairs, haven't you?"

His eyelids dropped to half-mast and he tilted his pink nose upward — it looked as if he were smiling at me. I continued to tickle him between the ears as I reached for the mail. The first letter I picked up was postmarked Palo City, California.

"Dawn!" I gasped. "She wrote me."

The letter was nice and thick, five pages front and back. If I couldn't talk to my stepsister and best friend, reading a letter from her was the next best thing.

Dawn wrote that Tuesday was a sunny, warmish day in California (which was a little hard to imagine, since there was still snow on the ground in Connecticut). The DeWitt boys, dressed in costumes, had been waiting for her in the front yard. . . .

"Hold, fair lady!" Erick yelled, hopping from behind a palm tree. "I am ready to slay yon dragon and bring you his head."

"Slay yon dragon!" Dawn gasped, putting one hand to her heart. "But who are you, sir?"

"I am Sir Launcelot!" Erick swept his long plastic sword in a grand motion and bowed. "At your service!"

When he bowed, the visor of his knight helmet fell shut over his eyes. As he struggled to adjust it, his armor came undone on the right shoulder and his chest plate flopped down across his tummy. Dawn had to turn away so Erick wouldn't see her laughing. When she looked back, she was met by a different kind of knight, from another century.

"Howdy, pardner!" Ryan cried, stepping out from behind another palm tree. He was astride his stick horse, the reins clutched in one hand and a silvery cap gun in the other. "I'm rescuing this here lady. Back off, knight!"

"Butt out, cowboy!" Erick yelled, jerking his visor up again, so he could see.

"Do you want me to fill you full of holes?" Ryan asked.

"I'll turn you into shish kabob," Erick shot back.

That's when Dawn held out her hands in a T. "Time! Time out!"

The boys lowered their weapons. "What's wrong?" Ryan asked innocently.

Dawn folded her arms across her chest. "First of all, you know I don't like guns, even toy guns. When I'm with you, I'd prefer that you didn't play with them."

Ryan's face fell. "Aw, this is my new Christmas present. I want to play with it."

Thinking fast, Dawn said, "But I'd really like to see your other presents, too. I know you got more, because I saw your tree. The gifts were stacked so high, they practically touched the ceiling."

Erick grabbed Dawn by the hand. "Come to my room. I'll show you mine."

Ryan grabbed her other arm. "Mine first."

"No, mine!" Erick cried, with a tug of Dawn's arm.

"Mine!" Ryan yanked back.

"Hey!" Dawn gasped. "Take it easy!"

"What are you boys doing?" Cynthia DeWitt

called from the front porch. "Trying to tear Dawn in two? Could you at least wait till I've left the house? Otherwise she'll change her mind and go home."

"Hi, Cynthia," Dawn called. "Happy New Year."

Normally we don't call our clients by their first names, but Cynthia DeWitt insists. She's an actress, and she looks like one: tall and slender, with huge brown eyes and a dazzling smile. Cynthia has done a ton of TV commercials. Toothpaste, soda, dish detergent, aspirin — you name it, she's sold it.

"Come inside before the Knights of the Kitchen Table tear you to pieces," Cynthia said, waving Dawn into her living room.

The DeWitts' living room is amazing. It's covered from floor to ceiling in photographs. There are Cynthia's and Mr. DeWitt's wedding shots, and honeymoon photos from the Far East. There are pictures of Cynthia in various costumes. Every family campout or trip is captured on film and framed in that room, too.

"I have an audition at Friedson/Alper Casting offices, and then I'll be doing a voice-over at Arctic Air Studios." Cynthia handed Dawn a piece of paper with the phone numbers on it. "I shouldn't be gone longer than a few hours, but in case I'm running late, I've made a quiche. Could you pop it in the oven around six?"

"Sure," Dawn said.

Cynthia turned to check her reflection in the mirror over the mantel. She adjusted the collar on her plaid blouse and smoothed her skirt. "This audition is for an aspirin commercial. What do you think? Do I look like a pleasant third-grade teacher with a headache?" Cynthia put one hand to her temple and winced.

"Perfect." Dawn laughed. "You'll land the part for sure."

"Thanks." Cynthia gave her hair one last pat, then turned to shout out the front door, "Boys, I'm leaving. You better give me a hug. For luck."

"Good luck, my lady," Erick the knight cried, galloping toward his mom.

"Hey, that's no lady!" Ryan the cowboy shouted. "That's my mother."

"Comedians." Cynthia chuckled as she hugged the two boys. "Everyone in this house is a comedian."

Then Cynthia planted big red kisses on the boys' foreheads, hopped in her Jeep Cherokee, and drove off. Dawn felt exhausted from the commotion, and her sitting job had just begun.

Once they were inside the house, Ryan and Erick drew straws to see who would show

Dawn his toys first. Erick won. But as soon he had shown her his castle and all the lords and ladies who lived there, he was ready to move on to something more fun. However, Ryan still wanted to show Dawn *his* toys.

"Dawn, could I go over to Corey McKinsey's house?" Erick asked.

Corey lives a block and a half away from the DeWitts. Erick often plays at his house and vice versa.

"I should phone Corey's mom first," Dawn replied.

"It's okay. Mom already called her," Erick said. "She said they'd be home all afternoon."

Dawn checked the clock. "Okay. You can go over for half an hour. And remember to call me as soon as you get to the McKinseys'."

After Erick left, Ryan eagerly displayed his treasures. Besides the cowboy outfit, he had received a Gator Golf game, a remote-controlled robot, and a new Super Nintendo game.

"Your parents must have cleaned out the toy store," Dawn said in amazement.

Ryan pushed his red cowboy hat off his forehead and nodded eagerly. "I'm already starting my list for next year."

The two of them had played only a couple of rounds of Gator Golf when Dawn heard the front door bang open. Moments later a very distraught Erick appeared in the bedroom.

"What's the matter?" Dawn gasped, running to him.

Eric was crying so hard he could hardly talk. He held out his hand. His palm was covered with blood. "I fell," he sobbed. "On a nail, I think. It hurts."

"Oh, my gosh!" Ryan cried, pointing to the blood dripping on the floor. "He's bleeding to death. Erick's bleeding! What do we do?"

Dawn took a deep breath, silently ordering herself to remain calm. The cut looked awful, but the last thing she wanted to do was frighten Erick by overreacting.

"Come on, Erick," she said, cupping her hand under his and gently leading him to the bathroom. "Let's wash that off. Then we can take a closer look at it."

"Am I going to die?" Erick asked through little hiccuping sobs.

"No, you are not going to die," Dawn said as she ran the palm of his hand under cold water. When the blood cleared, she could see where the nail had punctured his palm. "But you're right, you did fall on a nail."

"It was a huge nail," Erick said, sniffing.

"You are so brave," she said, speaking in her most calming voice. Then over her shoulder she called to Ryan, who was watching from the bathroom door, pale with fright.

"Ryan? Would you please find the first-aid kit? I think it's in that cupboard by the door."

Ryan nodded and did what he was told. "Do you want a Band-Aid?" he asked, setting the box on the bathroom counter.

"Eventually," Dawn said. "First we want to make sure the bleeding's stopped." She found a large gauze pad and pressed it against Erick's palm. "I'm going to raise your arm above your head," she explained to Erick, "because we need to stop the bleeding. Then we can put a Band-Aid on it."

Luckily Dawn has taken a first-aid course. All of us have. It was Kristy's idea, and the information we learned has come in handy more than once for all of us in the Baby-sitters Club.

Dawn told Erick to sit on a chair in the kitchen. He had finally stopped crying but was still shaken by the accident. Ryan followed, carrying the first-aid kit.

"Ryan, you're being a great helper," Dawn said. "Will you do me one more favor?"

"Do you want me to call an ambulance?" Ryan asked, his eyes still large with fear. "I can dial nine-one-one."

"I don't think an ambulance will be necessary," Dawn answered, hiding a smile. "But I think your brother could use a glass of juice. He's had a shock."

"All right." Ryan bolted for the refrigerator.

"Okay, Erick." Dawn handed him a tissue to wipe his tears and blow his nose. "Tell me exactly what happened and where."

He had calmed down a little and could talk more clearly. "I was going to Corey's and I decided to take the shortcut through that vacant lot by the Huffmans'."

Dawn nodded. "I know that spot. It's a disaster. Some people throw their trash there."

Erick nodded. "It's a total garbage dump. I was jumping over a pile of boards in the middle, and I guess I caught my shoe on a piece of wire. The next thing I knew I was falling forward. I put out my arms, and something jabbed into my hand. A big nail."

"I'll bet it was a rusty nail," Dawn murmured.

Erick nodded.

"Whoever owns that lot ought to be sued or something," Dawn grumbled. "It's a dangerous eyesore in the middle of a great neighborhood. I'm not surprised you got hurt."

Dawn lowered Erick's arm. The bleeding had stopped, but the puncture looked bad. She thought Erick would probably need a tetanus shot, if he hadn't had one recently.

Erick watched her face as she examined his wound. "What do you think?" he asked.

"The bleeding has stopped, but I'm a little

concerned about that nail. If it was rusty, the cut could become infected." Dawn put a Band-Aid on Erick's palm. "I think your doctor ought to take a look at this."

"A doctor?" Erick gulped.

Dawn nodded. "Just to be on the safe side."

Ryan helped Dawn stack some books on the table so Erick could keep his hand elevated. Then Dawn gave the boys more juice and some saltine crackers. She remembered her mother used to feed her saltines when she was sick.

While the boys munched the crackers and drank their juice, Dawn made some phone calls. First she dialed Friedson/Alper Casting, but Cynthia had just left. Dawn figured it would be at least twenty minutes before Cynthia reached her next destination, so she decided to try to find Mr. DeWitt. He had stepped out of his office.

The next half hour was a blur of phone calls. Dawn even tried to reach her stepmother, Carol, to see if she could give them a ride to the doctor's, but Carol was out, too. Finally Dawn remembered that Corey's mom, Mrs. McKinsey, was home and had a car.

"Of course I'll drive you," Mrs. McKinsey said, after Dawn had explained the situation. "That lot has just been getting worse and worse. I'm declaring it off-limits to my kids."

While they waited for Mrs. McKinsey to pick them up, Dawn wrote a note to Mr. DeWitt, in case he arrived home before they returned. She called and left a message for Cynthia at the recording studio, then phoned the doctor's number posted on the refrigerator to let them know she was bringing Erick into the office.

During the car ride, Dawn worried about Erick, and thought about that vacant lot. Mrs. McKinsey was right in declaring it off-limits to her kids. But something more needed to be done. That owner, whoever he or she was, needed to clean it up.

When they reached the doctor's office, Cynthia DeWitt was already there. She had received the message at the recording studio and hurried straight over. It turned out that Erick did need a tetanus shot. Dawn was relieved that she had made the right decision.

That night, Dawn couldn't wait to call Sunny Winslow, one of the members of their baby-sitting club, the We ♥ Kids Club.

"Sunny, all of the kids we baby-sit for either play in that lot or walk through it. I think we need to do something about it."

"You're right," Sunny agreed. "But what?"

"I don't know. We'll have to think of something."

Dawn ended her letter on a happier note:

And that's all the news from California. I'll keep you posted about the lot. And if you have any brilliant ideas, write or call and let me know. I've gotta run. I think I have writer's cramp.

Much love,
Dawn

CHAPTER 7

Dawn's letter was the only bright spot in a terrible day. I didn't exactly feel cheery reading it but at least it took my mind off Amelia for a little while.

I carefully folded the letter and tucked it in my purse. Then I went upstairs to wash my face. When I looked in the mirror I had a shock. My eyes looked bloodshot, and the little bit of mascara I had hurriedly applied that morning had become two smudgy streaks down my cheeks.

Normally I would have been mortified that anyone had seen me looking like that, but this had not been a normal day. Staring at my reflection in the glass, I wondered if any day would ever feel normal again. A friend, who had been so alive less than twenty-four hours ago, was now gone forever. It was hard for me to accept.

Judging from Kristy's behavior at the BSC

meeting that afternoon, she was having trouble accepting it, too.

Logan walked with me to the meeting. We arrived five minutes early, but everyone else was already there and caught up in a very intense discussion.

"Amelia was so young," Kristy was saying as Logan and I came in. "She had her whole life ahead of her." Kristy's chin quivered as she spoke and tears filled her eyes. "It just isn't fair!"

Usually Kristy is the strong one and I'm the weeper. But she looked especially vulnerable that afternoon. Her cheeks were blotchy and her nose was running.

"What makes me so angry," Stacey said, "is that guy who hit them didn't even have a license."

Claudia nodded. "I heard on the radio that he'd been stopped four times for drunk driving and the police had taken away his license."

"They should have thrown him in jail!" Abby, whose father had died in a car crash, slammed her fist on the desk. "How could he get four chances to kill someone?"

"He's in jail now," Stacey reported. "And I hope he stays there forever."

"I just feel so helpless," I said, sitting on

Claudia's bed. "I wish there was something we could do about this."

Logan dropped onto the floor next to Mal and Jessi. "There are some things we can do about it," he said. "We can write letters to the newspaper. We can join S.A.D.D., Students Against Driving Drunk."

"I've heard of Mothers Against Drunk Driving," Stacey said, "but not S.A.D.D. What is it?"

"Well, I don't know that much about it," Logan admitted. "I just remember in Kentucky, when a boy at the high school was hit by a drunk, pamphlets suddenly started appearing all over town. Especially at the local student hangouts. They mostly listed statistics. It was pretty amazing. Drunk driving is an enormous problem."

"We don't need a pamphlet to know that," Kristy mumbled.

"The organization was started to educate teens about the dangers of driving under the influence of alcohol," Logan continued. "And to inform kids about the consequences you face if you do cause an accident."

"*What* consequences?" Abby threw her hands in the air. "That guy had his license taken away from him and he was still driving. They should have taken away his car."

"At least he's in jail now," I said. "Where he belongs."

Claudia nodded. "We should write the police. And let them know we think they should keep him locked up."

"But that won't bring Amelia back," Jessi reminded us.

"No," Kristy said, blowing her nose. "But it'll stop him from killing someone else. I mean, next time it could be one of us. Or one of the kids we sit for." Her chin began to quiver again. "I still can't believe Amelia's gone!"

"Her poor parents," I murmured. "They must be devastated."

"What about Josh?" Mallory said, pushing her glasses up on her face. "Has anybody heard how he's doing?"

"I heard he has a broken arm and some cuts on his face, from broken glass," Jessi said. "But he should be able to come back to school soon."

Mallory winced. "He's in most of my classes. What'll I say to him?"

Claudia cocked her head. "What do you mean?"

"Should I mention Amelia, or would he rather not talk about it?"

Jessi nodded. "I have Josh in a few of my

classes, too. It's going to be hard to face him."

"And what about Barbara Hirsch?" I added. "She's Amelia's best friend. What on earth will I say to her?"

"You just tell Josh or Barbara you're sorry and that you'll miss Amelia," Abby said, her lips a tight line. I think she was remembering when her father died.

Claudia nodded and clasped Abby's hand. "I know it meant a lot to me when people talked about Mimi. And it felt weird if someone didn't say anything about her — almost as if they didn't care."

Mallory shuddered. "I'd hate to have Josh think we didn't care. I just feel so awkward saying I'm sorry."

"You may feel awkward, but Josh will appreciate it," Abby reassured Mallory.

We sat for a moment in silence. Abby and Claudia were the only ones who had experienced losing a relative. (I'd lost my mom, but I was too little to remember it.) That moment of silence was for Abby and Claud.

"I wish there were something we could do for Amelia." Kristy blew her nose again and looked at us with watery eyes. "But what can we do?"

"Maybe we could do something to help remember her," I suggested.

"Like what?" Kristy asked miserably.

"Well, the funeral is Monday," Stacey pointed out. "Maybe we could send flowers or something."

Kristy just nodded.

Stacey checked the manila envelope where she keeps the club dues. "We were going to use this money to buy supplies for our Kid-Kits, but I think this is much more important."

"I agree," Claudia said. "I vote we send flowers. We can call the florist today."

At this point, Kristy, as club president, would usually have asked for a show of hands to make sure we were in agreement. But she hardly seemed aware of what we were discussing.

"Should we send a card?" Jessi asked. "With the flowers?"

"I think the florist usually puts a card with the flowers," Claudia said. "But if you like, I could draw one, and we could all sign it over the weekend."

"That would be wonderful," I said.

Once again, we took an informal vote, while Kristy just stared at her hands.

"Is there anything else?" Mallory asked. "I have no idea what you're supposed to do when someone dies."

74

"That's because kids our age don't normally die," Logan pointed out.

His words seemed to hang in the air, as once again we tried to absorb the reality that our friend was gone.

I thought about my study group for English, and how we were now one person short. That's when I had the idea to dedicate our project to Amelia. If she couldn't be there in body, at least we would have her with us in spirit.

I pulled a piece of lined paper from the back of the BSC notebook and made a note to myself to talk to Gordon and Barbara about the dedication.

Brring!

The phone rang three times, which was probably a club first. Everyone in the room was so miserable that no one moved to answer the phone.

"Kristy, you're nearest," Claudia finally said. "Why don't you pick it up?"

Kristy stared at Claudia, as though she didn't quite understand.

Brring!

The phone rang one more time. Finally, Kristy noticed it. "Hello?" she answered.

Stacey and Claudia frowned at each other. Kristy always, *always* answers the phone by saying, "Hello, Baby-sitters Club."

"Oh. Yes," Kristy continued. "This is the Baby-sitters Club. Hello, Mrs. Hobart. . . . No, this is Kristy."

She listened for a few more seconds. Then she hung up and stared at the rug.

"Kristy?" I asked gently. "Does Mrs. Hobart need a sitter?"

Kristy blinked at me. "Yes. For Saturday."

"Do you know what time?"

Kristy nodded. "Seven o'clock."

As I said, Kristy is the most outgoing, outspoken member of the club. And usually nothing is as important to her as the Baby-sitters Club and making sure it stays ship-shape. But now she could barely concentrate on it.

"Do you want to lie down or something, Kristy?" I asked.

She shook her head. "I'm not ill. It's just so . . . so sad, about Amelia." Kristy bit her lip, trying hard not to burst into tears. "Why Amelia? What did she do to deserve this?"

This was very weird. Amelia and Kristy were friends, but not close friends. In fact, I knew Amelia better than Kristy did. I could understand why Kristy was upset that someone our age had died. But I couldn't understand why Kristy was having more trouble than the rest of us accepting the bad news.

"We better call Mrs. Hobart," Jessi reminded us. "She's waiting to hear about a sitter."

"Right." I checked the schedule book. "Hmm . . ." Kristy was free, but she didn't seem to be in any condition to accept a job. The rest of us were booked, or not available.

"Looks like it's you," I said to Logan with a smile. "Can you do it?"

He shrugged. "Sure. An evening with the Hobarts is always an adventure."

He was referring to the fact that the Hobarts have three boys. Well, actually four boys, but Ben is in Mal's and Jessi's class, and no longer needs a sitter. (In fact, Ben often sits for his younger brothers.) The other Hobarts — James, Mathew, and Johnny — can be a handful. An evening with them usually involves arm and leg wrestling and lots of running. Come to think of it, Logan was probably the perfect sitter for them.

During the rest of the meeting, I kept a careful eye on Kristy. She just wasn't herself. At one point, Claudia passed around a bag of chocolate stars. Kristy turned it down and passed the bag to me with shaking hands.

I made a vow, right then and there, to look after Kristy. She has always been the strong one in our friendship, speaking up for me in groups, making sure my feelings (which bruise easily) don't get hurt, and in general being a terrific best friend. Now it was time for me to take care of Kristy.

I took a deep breath. That meant being extra strong, which was going to be hard. I hoped I was up to the job.

CHAPTER 8

"Sharon? Do you have a black blouse I can borrow?"

It was Monday morning. The night before, I'd rifled through my closet trying to find something black to wear to Amelia's funeral. All I could manage was an old, slightly faded black turtleneck and some black slacks. Pants didn't feel right at all, so I called Stacey. She loaned me a black skirt, but my faded turtleneck looked terrible with it.

Sharon appeared in my door with several blouses on hangers and a sweater. "Mary Anne, I have a few things that might do, but you don't *have* to wear black to a funeral, you know."

"You don't?"

I'd attended Claudia's grandmother's funeral, but that event had become a blur in my memory. All I could think of to wear to my classmate's funeral was black, like in the movies.

"Something dark-colored or conservative would be just fine," Sharon said. "Like your navy blue plaid skirt and a sweater. That would be very appropriate."

I went to my closet for what must have been the thirteenth time. "Maybe you're right," I murmured. "I think I'd feel much better in my own clothes."

Sharon came into the room and sat on my bed, watching me. "Mary Anne, I know this has been a tough time for you. How are you holding up?"

"Fine," I said without really thinking about my answer. I chose a sweater that looked nice with my plaid skirt and laid them both on the bed next to Sharon.

She put her hand on my arm. "Truthfully?"

"Truthfully?" I looked into her eyes. "I have my ups and downs." I pushed the clothes out of the way and slumped next to Sharon. "Like this weekend, I would sometimes go for several hours without thinking about Amelia. Then all of a sudden it would hit me that I hadn't thought about her, and I'd feel incredibly guilty."

"Why guilty?"

"I'm not sure. I guess because I really liked

Amelia and to forget about her so easily seems terrible."

"But you're not forgetting Amelia," Sharon reminded me. "When she was alive, there were lots of times you didn't think about her, and that was okay, wasn't it?"

"Yes."

"It's still okay, now that she's gone." Sharon wrapped her arms around me and hugged me close. "Oh, Mary Anne, I know what you're going through. I lost a close friend when I was just a few years older than you. Her name was Jane Townsend. I think I walked around like a zombie for nearly a month after Jane died."

"Then what happened?" I asked.

"Life went on. That didn't mean I'd forgotten Jane. Quite the opposite. I thought of her a lot. A few times, something really funny would happen and I'd think, 'Jane has got to hear this.' I'd rush to the phone to call her, but by the time I touched the receiver I'd remember that she wasn't there anymore. And I'd want to cry."

I looked up and saw that Sharon's eyes were starting to mist over. She gave me a sad smile. "Life has gone on, but Jane is still with me in my memory. She always will be."

I suddenly felt this huge lump in my throat. Sharon had been very supportive over the weekend. Dad, too. They'd canceled their dinner plans just to be home in case I wanted to talk with them. I hadn't felt much like talking, but that was okay, too. They just wanted me to know that they were there when I needed them.

Logan had also been wonderful. We'd shared a winter picnic at Carle playground on Sunday. He told me funny stories about his sitting job with the Hobarts. They had built a fort that covered the living room, dining room, and kitchen. They must have used every blanket, sheet, and tablecloth in the house. Then they had talked Logan into crawling through it while they made scary sounds.

"It was my first haunted fort," Logan told me with a laugh. "Afterward, we ate graham crackers and peanut butter inside the fort, while the kids told ghost stories. We couldn't have had more fun if we'd planned it."

After my picnic with Logan, Dad drove me to Kristy's house. I wanted to see how she was doing. I found Kristy sitting on the couch in the living room, wrapped in a blanket. A box of Kleenex sat on the floor beside the couch, and our seventh grade yearbook was open on her lap.

"Are you sick?" I asked, sitting cross-legged on the carpet in front of the couch.

"I don't have a cold, if that's what you

mean." Kristy's voice was listless and tired. "I've just been looking at pictures of Amelia from last year."

Kristy turned the book for me to see. There was a photo of Amelia in the talent show with Barbara. They were dressed as Raggedy Ann and Andy, flashing big grins at the audience.

"I remember that," I said, smiling at the memory. "They did that floppy dance. Amelia was really funny."

Kristy flipped ten pages ahead. (It was clear she'd spent a lot of time with this yearbook.) "Here's Amelia on Earth Day. Remember? She and Dawn were the main organizers of that event."

The picture showed Amelia working at a booth under a sign that read *Daily Planet*. She was handing out a brochure about recycling to a sixth-grader.

I stared at Amelia's picture. Two other girls were standing behind her. I tried to find something in Amelia's face that singled her out from the others. Something that would explain why she would be the one killed in a car accident. But she looked just like everyone else.

"Look at her," Kristy said, tugging a tissue out of the box. "She was a leader. She had her whole future ahead of her." Kristy dabbed at the corners of her eyes. "It just doesn't make any sense."

I forced myself to remember my vow to be strong for Kristy. But it was hard. I wanted to curl up beside her and cry, too.

Kristy was trying to work through something. Amelia's death and something more. But I wasn't quite sure what that something was. I did a lot of listening that afternoon.

By Sunday night, I felt drained. I didn't even have enough energy to read a book or watch TV. I fell into bed and was asleep within minutes.

On Monday, after I'd finally chosen my outfit for the funeral, Sharon drove me to school. The funeral was at eleven. Lots of kids were planning to go to their first three classes, then walk to the First Methodist Church, which was only a few blocks from SMS.

At school, the bells rang indicating the beginning and ending of classes, just like any other day. But no one was acting as though it were a normal day. Most of the students milled around in the halls, waiting.

I went to Mr. Blake's homeroom, and part of another class, but I was having trouble concentrating on anything but the funeral.

As eleven o'clock drew closer, I started to feel butterflies in my stomach. It was the same feeling I had whenever I was supposed to give a report in front of class — major fear.

I think I was afraid of doing something really

embarrassing or wrong at the funeral. What if I suddenly lost control and couldn't stop weeping? What if I fainted?

By ten o'clock, I'd worked myself into such a panic about attending the funeral and making a fool of myself in front of the entire student body that I decided I needed to talk to someone about it. I made myself go down to the guidance office the next period, where I asked to speak to a grief counselor.

A woman named Kathleen listened carefully as I described my fears. She had warm, brown eyes and a pleasant face. I told her that I had been to a funeral before but never for someone my own age. I was afraid how I might react. When I stopped talking, she took my hand and held it.

"All of those fears are normal," Kathleen assured me. "You're not sure how you should behave at a friend's funeral, and you're embarrassed about it. Most of the students at this school probably haven't attended a funeral before. They're all feeling as awkward and worried as you are."

Talking to Kathleen did make me feel a little better about the funeral. But nothing could have prepared me for what lay ahead.

At ten-thirty, I met Logan and Kristy at my locker. Claudia, Stacey, Abby, Mallory, and Jessi joined us in the schoolyard, along with everyone else at SMS. The entire student body and all of the teachers walked quietly to the First Methodist Church. It must have been an impressive sight to see so many kids, dressed in somber colors, moving quietly through the streets of Stoneybrook.

We could hear organ music as we climbed the steps to the church entrance. The rich scent of roses filled the church. In the vestibule stood an easel holding a framed photo of Amelia. It was her class picture. I realized I had a wallet-size version in my purse.

Kristy and I reached for each other's hands. A tight knot formed in my chest. "Look how beautiful she is," I whispered to Kristy and Logan.

Logan nodded sadly. When we entered the sanctuary and I saw the mahogany coffin — Amelia's coffin — surrounded by pink and white flowers, my heart did a flip-flop.

For a second my knees went wobbly. I was glad Logan was beside me. He caught my elbow and guided me toward an empty pew five rows from the front of the church.

The eight of us filled half a row. No one spoke. We sat numbly, staring at the coffin as the other mourners filed into pews around us. When the church was filled, more people found places to stand by the windows. They jammed the aisles and overflowed onto the sidewalks outside. It felt good to know Amelia had had so many friends.

I read later in the *Stoneybrook News* that over a thousand people attended Amelia's funeral, including representatives from Students Against Driving Drunk. They'd come from Stamford to show their support for the Freemans.

At ten after eleven, Reverend Downey appeared, along with the Freeman family. Seeing them was almost too much to bear. They still showed the effects of the accident. Josh's arm was in a cast, and his face was covered with bruises. Mr. Freeman had a large bandage on his forehead, and Mrs. Freeman was on crutches. They looked as if the world had defeated them.

When they were seated, Reverend Downey began the service. "We gather here today to celebrate the memory of Amelia Louise Freeman."

Louise. It occurred to me that I had never known Amelia's middle name. I knew she was thirteen and that her birthday was in September, but not that her middle name was Louise.

Reverend Downey mentioned many other things about Amelia that I'd never heard before. I hadn't known that she played the piano. I never knew her favorite movie had been *The Secret Garden*. Or that she had a stuffed rabbit named Nibs that she had slept with since she was a baby.

And now I would never know any more about her, except what I heard from other people.

The ache in my chest spread, filling my body with a sadness. Tears streamed down my cheeks.

Reverend Downey tried to focus the service on remembering happy days with Amelia. But all I could think about was the unfairness of life.

How was it possible that an irresponsible drunk could cause an accident, kill a perfectly innocent girl — and walk away almost without a scratch? There seemed to be no justice in the world.

When the service finally ended, a violinist played "Amazing Grace" from the rear of the church. It was the most haunting sound I ever heard.

As the violinist played, I looked around the church. So many young faces. And each shining face streaked with tears.

"Good-bye," I whispered when the last notes faded away. "I'll really miss you."

CHAPTER 9

"Barbara's back," Stacey whispered to me Tuesday morning. "I saw her talking to Josh before homeroom."

"Did you say anything to her?" I asked.

Stacey shook her head. "I didn't know what to say. They were both standing there. I mean, do I tell Josh I'm sorry about Amelia, and then say the same thing to Barbara?"

"So what did you do?"

Stacey stared at the floor. "I turned and walked the other way."

"Don't worry about it," I said, patting her on the arm. "They probably didn't notice."

"They had to," Stacey said. "I think every student in homeroom either did an about face or pretended not to see them. It was pretty obvious."

"Poor Josh and Barbara," I replied.

"I know," Stacey said with a grimace. "I promise I won't do it again. The next time I run into them, I'll at least say hi."

I decided to do more than that. I'd talk to them. But my chance came before I was totally prepared.

Just as I was about to enter math class, I spotted Josh in the hall. He seemed so alone and dejected.

"Josh!" I called. "Wait up."

He looked up at me, but his expression didn't change.

"How are you doing?" I asked, touching his shoulder.

Josh just shrugged.

I took a deep breath and spoke really fast. "Josh, I just want you to know how sorry I am about your sister. Everyone liked her, and we're all going to miss her."

Josh stared at me for a few moments, his blue eyes clouded with sadness. Then he burst into tears. I was so startled, I didn't know what to do. His books tumbled to the floor but he didn't seem to notice. He just stood in the middle of the hall, sobbing.

I glanced nervously around for a teacher or counselor, somebody to help me. Even though the bell hadn't rung, the halls were deserted.

"Josh," I said, picking up his books and gently taking him by the arm. "Do you want to talk to Mrs. Amer?"

Josh shook his head, continuing to sob.

That did it. I wrapped my arms around him and hugged him tight. It was the best thing I could do. Even after the bell rang, we stood there like that.

Finally Josh raised his head. "I think I better go home," he managed to say.

I ushered Josh to the front office and sat with him while the secretary called his mother.

Ten minutes later, his mother picked him up. Josh, who hadn't said a word while we waited, turned his tear-streaked face to me and whispered, "Thanks, Mary Anne."

My heart ached for Josh. Still, I was glad that I was able to be there for him. If I couldn't help Amelia, at least I had helped her brother.

I asked the secretary for a late pass and as I headed for my next class, I thought about what Sharon had told me: "Life goes on." It was true. Today the students were dressed in their usual bright, colorful clothes. The grief counselors were gone. Classes were back to normal.

Or at least they appeared to be normal. In Mrs. Simon's English class, we were all acutely aware of Amelia's absence. Hers was the only empty desk in the room. And sitting next to it was Barbara Hirsch.

"Class," Mrs. Simon said as she passed out paper, "I thought, rather than starting with a specific play, we would read some of Shakespeare's wonderful speeches. The opening speech from *Henry V* is a perfect introduction to our visit with Mr. Bill."

Mrs. Simon paused at Barbara's desk and asked her how she was doing.

"Not very well," Barbara answered truthfully. "I think I'm still in shock."

Mrs. Simon patted Barbara's shoulder gently. "Just let me know if you want to talk."

Barbara nodded.

Then Mrs. Simon stepped to the front of the class and explained a few of the phrases that we would be hearing in the first speech. "Our narrator, or Chorus as he is called in the play, asks us to use our imagination to picture everything that happens within 'this wooden O.' Does anyone know what he means by that — a wooden O?"

I automatically looked toward Amelia's desk. So did a few other students. She, of any of us, would have known the answer.

When no one raised a hand, Mrs. Simon explained, "He's referring to Shakespeare's theatre, the Globe Theatre, which was essentially a three-story wooden structure in the shape of an O."

She pointed to a painting of the Globe Theatre, then unveiled a dollhouse-size model on her desk.

After giving us a chance to come to her desk

and look the model over, Mrs. Simon showed us a costume doublet she said had been worn by a famous actor from a theatre company that used to be in Connecticut. By the time she was ready to read the speech, we were prepared to listen. She asked us to close our eyes and then she began.

"Oh, for a muse of fire, that would ascend the brightest heaven of invention . . ."

Pictures of kings and knights in armor, astride beautiful horses on the fields of France, filled my brain, replacing all the sad thoughts that had been there. It felt wonderful just to relax and imagine.

Ten minutes before the class came to an end, Mrs. Simon told us to split into our groups and work on our projects. Then she called Barbara, Gordon, and me up to her desk.

"I realize that this is a difficult time for you," she said, perching on the corner of her desk. "If you would like to change your project to something less taxing, for three people, that would be fine with me."

Gordon looked at Barbara, and then at me. I shook my head. "No," I said to Mrs. Simon. "We have a great project that's filled with a lot of Amelia's ideas."

Barbara pursed her lips. "I think we should do it for Amelia."

Gordon agreed.

That's when I made my suggestion. "I propose that we dedicate our project to Amelia."

"What a splendid idea!" Mrs. Simon said. Gordon agreed.

Barbara smiled as her eyes filled with tears. "That's a really nice thought, Mary Anne. I second it."

It was settled. I felt good that we would be able to create our own small memorial to our friend.

By the time I reached the cafeteria, I was actually smiling. Logan met me in the lunch line, and I told him what my group had decided to do.

"That's a great idea," he said. "Maybe it will help you feel better." He gestured with his thumb toward the table where Kristy was sitting. "I wish something would make Kristy feel better. She's obsessed with this drunk driver and what he did."

As if in response to his words, Kristy pounded the cafeteria table with her fist. I couldn't hear what she was saying to Claudia, but it was obvious that Kristy was upset and angry about something.

Logan and I moved down the cafeteria line, where we joined Abby, who announced in a loud voice, "Oh look, folks, it's my favorite food — mystery meat on toast."

I decided to skip the main course and have a chef's salad instead. Logan opted for a carton of yogurt. Abby reluctantly chose the chicken noodle soup. "They probably put mystery meat in here, too," she declared grumpily. "Let's hope I don't have a reaction." (I told you she's allergic to everything.)

"He's a cold-blooded murderer," Kristy was saying as we arrived at the table.

"Let me guess," Abby said. "We're talking about that drunk."

Kristy hit the table again. "He makes me so mad. I just wish there was something I could do about it."

"Maybe there is something we can do," I said slowly. An idea that had been floating in the back of my mind suddenly took shape. "Maybe we could start our own chapter of Students Against Driving Drunk."

Kristy froze with her mouth half open and her finger pointing in mid-air. She turned slowly to face me, her eyes wide.

"You're right!" she whispered. "They fight drunk driving, don't they?"

"It would be pretty easy to start up," Logan added. "They have a number in the book. You just call them and ask how to do it."

"Our club would be huge," Kristy said, opening her arms wide. "There must have

95

been three hundred students at the funeral. I bet at least half of them would like to do something about drunk drivers."

"Uh-oh," Claudia murmured, taking a sip of her cola. "Kristy's getting that *look* in her eye again. That means we're going to be working day and night on her new project."

Kristy actually grinned at that. "It'll be worth it. Just think, Claud, if we were able to put more of these drunks behind bars, then they'd be off the streets. And more lives would be saved."

Stacey arrived at our table, carrying a tray with salad and apple slices.

"You're just in time to join Kristy's new club," Abby greeted her.

"New club?" Stacey repeated.

"This isn't a baby-sitting club," Kristy explained, her voice rising with excitement. "This is a club to keep drunk drivers off the streets. We're starting our own chapter of Students Against Driving Drunk."

"Sign me up," Stacey said firmly.

"Now all we need is the school's approval," I said.

"There's one of the guidance counselors." Logan pointed to Mr. Seitz, a blond man setting his empty tray in the dirty dish rack. "Why don't you talk to him?"

Kristy didn't hesitate. She was out of her

seat and across the cafeteria like a shot. I hurried to join her.

Mr. Seitz listened carefully to our idea. "I'm all for it," he said. "I'll talk to Mrs. Amer, and we'll contact the national office and ask them to send some of their literature."

For the remainder of the lunch period, Kristy talked nonstop about the new club — how to publicize it, when to have our first meeting, what the club could accomplish. The ideas just poured out of her.

I was thrilled. It looked as if the old Kristy Thomas might be back.

CHAPTER 10

Saturday

Dear Mary Anne,

Great news! (Finally, after the really sad news about Amelia) I, Dawn Schafer, am heading the coolest project in Southern California. Okay, it wasn't my idea, but I recognized it as great and ran with it. (Kristy would have been proud of me.) Remember that vacant lot that was a major health hazard? Well, that's all changed. As of this writing, it is about to become "a thing of beauty"....

A letter from Dawn. Hooray! I raced from the mailbox into the house, tore open the envelope, and paused. Something very furry was rubbing around my ankles.

"Tigger, I didn't say hello to you." I scooped him into my arms and buried my face in his fur. "Dawn wrote us a letter. Shall we read it together?"

Tigger raised his nose to look at me, then rubbed his face along my chin.

"I take that as a yes," I said, nuzzling him between the ears. His eyelids dropped to half mast and I knew if Tigger could talk, he would be purring, "Heaven."

I carried Tigger, in his blissful kitten state, into the kitchen and cuddled him while I brewed a cup of tea. I intended to make the reading of this letter a real event. Dawn and I had talked on the phone several times since Amelia's death. We'd shared a lot of memories of Amelia and shed quite a few tears. Those had been sad conversations. I was hoping her letter held cheery news.

When the water was boiling, I placed two of Sharon's granola cookies, along with several apple slices, on a china plate and carried it into the living room.

Tigger and I curled up in the armchair and

shared a cookie as I carefully unfolded Dawn's letter.

This one continued the saga of the dangerous lot. It involved Sunny Winslow, Dawn's best friend in California. I should tell you a little about Sunny. She has strawberry blonde hair and freckles across her upturned nose, and a great tan. Sunny's a health food nut like Dawn. But she's more like Kristy in personality — outgoing, fun, and independent — which makes her the perfect person to head the We ♥ Kids Club.

The We ♥ Kids Club is a baby-sitting club, but it isn't much like ours. The BSC has strict rules and regulations. They don't. We meet regularly three times a week at exactly the same time. They meet when they feel like it (though they do try to have at least one meeting a week). We have officers and keep a notebook. They don't. They *do* have an appointment book and they *do* use Kid-Kits. But that's about it.

Anyway, Dawn was looking after Stephie Robertson, who's eight, and Sunny was next door sitting for the Austin girls, five-year-old Clover and eight-year-old Daffodil. It was another gorgeous day in California, so Dawn phoned Sunny at the Austins'.

"It's too great a day to stay inside," she

declared. "Why don't we take the kids for a walk?"

"You don't have to twist my arm," Sunny replied. "Meet you outside in two minutes."

The two minutes was to allow the Austin kids time to go to the bathroom, and to smear on sunblock.

Dawn used the time to make sure she had all of Stephie's medical supplies. Stephie has asthma, just like Abby. She goes through periods when her bronchial tubes close up, and she has trouble breathing. She needs her inhalator with her at all times, as well as her pills, just in case she has an asthma attack. Sometimes an asthma attack can be brought on by too much physical exertion, but a person can even have one while he sleeps!

"Yo! Dawn!" Sunny called from the front lawn a few minutes later. "We don't have all day!"

Dawn tucked Stephie's medicine into her fanny pack along with a small carton of juice, so Stephie could swallow her pills if she did have an attack.

"All right," Dawn said as they stepped outside. "Is everyone ready for our power walk?"

"Let's do it," Sunny said, marching toward the sidewalk. Clover and Daffodil had to jog to keep up with her.

Although Daffodil is the older of the two Austins, she's quieter and less physical than her sister. Clover is a powerhouse of energy. She barrels through life at the top of her lungs.

Clover charged in front of Sunny, doing cartwheels down the sidewalk. Then she hopped backward on one foot.

As the group passed the vacant lot, Dawn called out a warning. "Stay clear of that lot, everyone. Erick hurt his hand so badly he had to get a tetanus shot."

"A shot?" Clover's eyes grew huge and she carefully moved to the far side of the sidewalk, as if the weeds might reach out and grab her.

"Look!" Daffodil pointed to the opposite corner of the lot. "Someone dumped their garbage here." She leaned forward, squinting at the remnants of a green trash bag. "There's old soup cans, and Kleenex and — ew, gross! some stinky old diapers." She pinched her nose. "P.U."

"I want to see," Stephie said, running ahead to join her friend. "Yuck!"

"Look over there." Daffodil pointed nervously at a pile of tree limbs. "Something's moving in there."

"Careful, kids," Dawn cautioned as she jogged up beside Daffodil. "It could be a coyote, or a raccoon, or a — "

"*Cat!*" everyone screamed as a scrawny

orange-and-white cat bolted across the field.

Stephie started to make weird snorting sounds and for a second Dawn was afraid she was having an asthma attack. But she was having a giggle attack. So were Clover and Daffodil. The three girls were bent over, holding their stomachs, laughing.

Normally Dawn would have joined in but the sight of the mounds of trash made her lose her sense of humor. "I can't believe how ugly this lot is."

"It's awful." Sunny shook her head in disgust. "And it's a real health hazard."

"I wish there were something we could do about it," Dawn complained, folding her arms across her chest. "But I don't even know who owns it."

"Maybe someone could put a fence around it," Daffodil suggested. "A really high one, so you wouldn't see the garbage."

"Someone should dig a deep, deep hole," Clover said. "Then all the garbage would just fall in."

"I wish this lot were a garden," Stephie murmured. "Like the one in *The Secret Garden*. Filled with beautiful flowers."

Dawn's eyes grew as big as saucers. She turned to Sunny and said, "A garden. What a great idea!"

"And easy to do."

Sunny was already making plans. "We would just need to clear away the debris, turn over the soil, and start planting seeds."

"Can I help?" Stephie asked. "I've always wanted a garden."

"Of course you can," Dawn said. "Everybody can help — Clover, Daffodil, the Clune girls. Maybe we can even talk Ryan and Erick DeWitt into helping."

The rest of the walk was a nonstop brainstorming session, with everyone, kids and sitters alike, tossing in ideas.

After their sitting jobs were over, Sunny stayed at Dawn's and they continued to make plans.

"First on our list is to find out the owner's name and address," Sunny said. "We'll talk to our parents and see if they can help us."

"Then we'll write him a straightforward letter," Dawn added. "Making sure not to insult him, but letting him know that the lot could be a health hazard if we don't clean it up."

Dawn's dad was enthusiastic about their project. He promptly made a few phone calls and in less than an hour, they had the owner's name, James L. Cruickshank, and his address, which was in Tucson.

Dawn typed the letter on her dad's computer, and fired it off to Arizona that very night.

It's amazing what you can do if you really put your mind to it. Sunny and Dawn contacted the other members of the We ♥ Kids Club, and together they started a phone chain, calling all the kids in the neighborhood.

Over the next few days, Dawn and Sunny gathered cleanup supplies, which consisted of thick gloves, rakes, and metal garbage cans. Each kid who'd been contacted was asked to bring one sturdy garbage bag to the lot on Friday afternoon.

Waiting for a letter to arrive can be agony. Dawn checked her mailbox every day, hoping to find a response from Mr. Cruickshank. And every day Sunny would call and have the same conversation with Dawn.

"Did he write?"

"No."

"Did he call?"

"Nope."

"Shoot. Well, maybe tomorrow."

By Friday afternoon, the scheduled day for the cleanup, they still hadn't heard a peep from Mr. Cruickshank.

At three-thirty, ten kids and their sitters were gathered on the sidewalk bordering the dirt lot. Dawn and Sunny realized they had to make a decision.

"I say we go ahead and start working," Dawn said firmly. "What's Mr. Cruickshank going to do — tell us to put the garbage back?"

"You're right," Sunny agreed. "How could he possibly object to a cleanup?"

Dawn blew the lifeguard whistle hanging from a blue cord around her neck. "All right, campers, we're going to form a line from the trash to the can. The sitters will pick up trash that is safe to handle and pass it to the kid next to them, who will pass it to the next kid — till it reaches the trash bag. Ready? Let's do it!"

Dawn's plan worked like a charm. Dawn and Sunny patrolled the lot, using heavy leather work gloves to pick up unsafe trash, such as boards with nails, sharp can lids, and broken glass. The other sitters gathered up the easy garbage, which passed from kid to kid into the waiting trash bags.

It couldn't have been a more orderly cleanup. They filled eighty-five giant trash bags that weekend. Dawn's stepmom Carol helped them take fifteen loads to the city dump. By Sunday night, Dawn's hands were blistered from raking and her back ached from hauling. But she didn't care.

Dawn ended her letter in triumph.

We did it. We really
cleaned up this town!
Love,
Dawn G. G.
(Garbage Girl)

CHAPTER 11

*B*rring!

Kristy dove for the phone on Watson's desk. "Students Against Driving Drunk, this is Kristy."

"Oops!" a voice on the other end of the line said. "I-I was looking for Sam Thomas. I think I must have — "

"Don't hang up," Kristy exclaimed. "This is Sam's house. It's also the headquarters for the Stoneybrook Chapter of S.A.D.D."

Headquarters was right. Watson had given Kristy the run of his home office while we launched the S.A.D.D. membership drive. We had a computer, a copier, a fax machine, and a file cabinet at our disposal.

It was incredible how quickly it had all come together. Mr. Seitz ordered a thousand brochures from the S.A.D.D. national office, and Mr. Kingbridge agreed to allow Stoneybrook Middle School to pay for the shipping.

Logan volunteered to distribute the bro- chures at a card table set up in front of the school entrance. He only had to sit there for a few days, because the brochures were snatched up in record time.

The phone rang again. This time the call was for S.A.D.D.

Kristy gave me a thumbs-up. "The first meeting will be next week," she told the caller. "I posted a sign-up sheet outside the main office today. . . . Great! I'll see you there, then." Kristy hung up the phone and pumped her fist in the air. "Yes!"

"That's the fifth call today," I said, checking my watch. "And we've only been home fifteen minutes. At this rate we're going to have a packed meeting."

Kristy nodded. "The brochures are working *and* — " Kristy spun in Watson's swivel chair and picked up a folded-up newspaper. "Take a look at this."

She handed me the latest issue of the *SMS Express*.

"Whoa," I gasped. "Emily gave us the entire front page."

Emily Bernstein is the editor of our school paper. She's a great person, but sometimes she can be a little stingy with her column space. Not that day.

"She did it for Amelia," Kristy explained. "She also told me to put her name on the list. She wants to be the first member of S.A.D.D."

I stared at the paper. The image of Amelia holding her stuffed rabbit, Nibs, smiled at me from the center of the page. Under the picture was an article titled, "Let's Do It for Amelia!" by Kristy Thomas.

I read the opening paragraph out loud.

"On January fourth, our friend, Amelia Freeman, became one of the more than seventeen thousand people killed each year by drunk drivers. It was a terrible tragedy, and one that could have been prevented. Students Against Driving Drunk is an organization dedicated to the proposition that kids can make a difference."

Brrring!

While Kristy answered the phone, I read the rest of her article. It was a good one, focusing on the importance of educating ourselves and our friends about the deadly combination of alcohol and cars, and what we could do to prevent more tragedies from occurring. The first meeting was slated for Friday. Kristy urged everyone to show their support by attending. The article ended with her new slogan, "Let's do it for Amelia!"

"Amelia," I murmured. As I stared down at

her face, a feeling of aching sadness over-whelmed me. Suddenly I realized tears were streaming down my cheeks.

Kristy didn't notice. She was too busy working the phone, spreading the word about S.A.D.D.

On Thursday Mr. Kingbridge let us make a short speech over the P.A. system during homeroom. Actually, Kristy spoke. (I told you I was shy.)

Kristy's sign-up sheet had been posted that morning and by lunchtime, the list was full.

"Mary Anne, check this out," Claudia called to me on our way to the cafeteria. "So many people signed up for S.A.D.D. they had to post another sheet."

"Kristy will be thrilled," I said. "We better think about finding a bigger room for the meeting."

Claudia shook her head in amazement. "This just goes to show you. Kids are mad and want to do something about it."

Mad was right. The announcement of the S.A.D.D. meeting had prompted another round of intense discussion about drunk drivers. Everywhere I turned — in the halls, at the cafeteria, on the front steps — kids were talking about it.

"A drunk driver is as much a criminal as

someone who takes a gun and shoots someone," Brian Hall was saying at lunch.

No one seemed to disagree with him.

That afternoon in gym class, I heard one sad story after another about friends and relatives who'd had collisions with drunk drivers. It was depressing.

By late afternoon, a third sign-up sheet had been filled.

Kristy was on cloud nine. I should have been, too, but for some reason, I wasn't. I just felt empty.

Logan noticed it on the way home from school. "Is something wrong?" he asked, cocking his head to look in my face. "You're awfully quiet."

"I feel sort of blue," I confessed.

"Was it math class?" he asked. "Did you have a test or something?"

"Actually it's funny you should ask," I said. "We did have a test today, and I think I aced it. Well, maybe not aced, but passed with a good solid B."

"All right!" Logan said, clapping his hands together. "We should celebrate. Why don't we go for a soda?"

I wanted to share his enthusiasm, but I could barely force myself to smile.

"Maybe I'm just tired," I said, rubbing my

eyes. "We've been working really hard on S.A.D.D., and my English project has been taking up a lot of time."

Logan's face fell. But he hid his disappointment. "Sounds like you could use a nap," he said. "We'll get a soda another time."

"Thanks, Logan," I said gratefully. "Maybe a nap would help."

I didn't really feel sleepy but after I said good-bye to Logan and entered my chilly empty house, all I wanted to do was lie down.

I stretched out on my bed and slept long and hard. I didn't wake up when Sharon or Dad came home. I didn't even wake up for dinner. It wasn't till eleven o'clock that night that I finally roused myself, just long enough to change into my pajamas and go back to bed.

The next morning Sharon and Dad were worried about me, but I assured them I wasn't ill, just exhausted.

That tired feeling stayed with me for the rest of the week. The least little thing could make me cry and when I wasn't feeling weepy, I just felt blah. I even felt that way during our S.A.D.D. meeting, when I should have been excited.

Kristy was pumped. She wore her good luck baseball cap with the picture of a collie on the front and a sweatshirt that the Stamford chapter of S.A.D.D. had given her.

Mr. Seitz had originally planned to let us use the teachers' conference room for the meeting, but so many kids showed up that we had to move into the auditorium.

Kristy looked right at home sitting on the stage with her legs dangling over the edge. She had wanted me to join her up front, but I couldn't do it. I told her I preferred to stand at the door. "That way I can greet late-comers," I said. What I didn't say was, that way no one will notice when I just stare at the walls.

The meeting was a monster success. Kids were throwing out suggestions right and left. Their enthusiasm was impressive. But some-how my attention kept wandering. I'd find myself staring into space until a voice would bring me back to the present.

"As I see it, we want to accomplish several things," Kristy was saying. "First, we want to get the word out that drunk driving is a major problem. So how do we do that?"

"I heard students in Stamford put a smashed car on display in front of their school."

I shuddered. That would be too hard to look at, especially so soon after Amelia's death.

"We could list names," one boy suggested.

"Paper the halls with the names of victims of drunk drivers."

"Great idea!" Kristy said. "Much more effective than listing numbers."

Ashley Wyeth, who once worked with Claudia at radio station WSTO, raised her hand. "We could tape public service announcements to run on local radio and TV stations urging teens not to drink or ride in a car with an impaired driver. We could state our name and age and then say that we lost our friend Amelia because of a drunk driver."

Claudia led the cheering for that idea.

Bea Foster raised her hand. "Why don't we bring in guest speakers? I heard that in Bridgeport, survivors of accidents come speak to classes. Their stories really seem to hit home."

Kristy nodded vigorously. Then she added, "The Stamford chapter gave me this shirt. Maybe we could order some more and sell them at school to raise money for the speakers."

Then Pete Black, president of the eighth grade, stood up. "I propose we have an S.A.D.D. awareness month. Each week we'll stage a special event, and all wear our shirts."

"I'll have our *Express* photographer take a picture," Emily Bernstein called out. "I'm sure we can get an article in the *Stoneybrook News*.

Maybe they'll go for a month-long feature."

Kristy gave her a thumbs-up. "Cool."

The longer the meeting went on, and the more students came up with better and better ideas for an S.A.D.D. awareness month, the more distant I felt from the meeting.

It was weird. I should have been thrilled. Instead, I was filled with a dull feeling of hopelessness and despair. I left before the meeting was over, slipping quietly out the side door. I knew Kristy would want to talk about the meeting. I just didn't feel up to it.

I walked home, slogging through the mushy brown snow. Without any leaves, the trees looked dead. Even the houses seemed to have been drained of their color. Why did everything seem so bleak?

Entering the house, I was hit with that overpowering feeling of wanting to lie down. I thought if I could just sleep I wouldn't feel so bad.

I don't know what it was that made me go into the kitchen, but I'm glad I did. Because on the bulletin board by the phone was a list of phone numbers and names. One name in particular seemed to leap out at me. Dr. Reese.

Dr. Reese is a therapist. She helps people work through their problems.

I have only told a few people this secret,

but not long ago, when Dad had just gotten married, and Logan and I were having some problems and my grades in English were dropping, I panicked.

I would wake up each morning and feel miserable. Then I'd spend the rest of the day worrying about what I'd said to Kristy, or Logan, or what someone had said to me. I agonized over everything I did.

Things grew worse and worse, and I started feeling tired all the time. It's a dead giveaway. It shows you want to hide from the world instead of face it.

I finally got up my courage and talked to my guidance counselor at school. She helped me confide in Dad, and he contacted Dr. Reese.

I saw the doctor after school for an hour each week. She helped me find out what was bothering me and learn how to cope with my problems. Dr. Reese was a lifesaver then, and seeing her name made me realize that she was just the person I needed to talk to now.

I knew Dad and Sharon would be supportive of my decision to see her again, so I didn't even hesitate.

I picked up the telephone and dialed her number.

"Dr. Reese's office," a pleasant voice answered.

I explained my situation to the receptionist. Dr. Reese had told me to call her any time I needed to talk, and she was on the phone in a flash. Within five minutes we had set up an appointment for me to see her after school on Monday.

CHAPTER 12

My heart thudded in my chest as I approached the new office building at the end of Main Street. Several dentists and an optometrist had their offices there, along with Dr. Reese.

Why should I feel nervous if I'd been to see the doctor before? Because even though I know that therapists can help you with your problems, a tiny part of me worries that I might be crazy.

Everything about Dr. Reese's outer office is designed to make you feel safe and comfortable. The dark green carpeting and leather chairs, along with the mahogany desk and bookshelves, make it look more like a living room than a waiting room.

I sank down in one of the big leather chairs and thumbed through a magazine as I waited for my name to be called. Classical music was playing softly from speakers on the book-shelves.

Less than five minutes had passed before I was ushered into Dr. Reese's office. She was sitting at her desk in her standard uniform of polo shirt, sweater, and chinos (yes, she's pretty preppy). Dr. Reese barely seems old enough to be a doctor, especially when she pulls her dark brown hair into a ponytail. She looks more like a college cheerleader or a camp counselor.

Anyway, it was good to see her.

"Mary Anne." She leaped up from her desk and gave me a warm hug. "Welcome."

All of my nervousness melted away and I remembered how good it felt being with Dr. Reese.

"I was just making some hot chocolate," she said, moving to the small microwave across from her desk. "Care to join me?"

"Sure," I said. "I think one of the last times I had hot chocolate was at your office."

Dr. Reese winked, "Don't tell anyone, but I'm addicted to the stuff. I'd drink it by the gallon if it weren't so fattening."

Where Dr. Reese's waiting room looks like a living room, her office is more like an old-fashioned sunporch. She has a chaise lounge upholstered in a cabbage rose pattern. That's where she sat, clutching her cup of hot chocolate. I curled up in a wingbacked chair covered in flowered chintz.

Dr. Reese opened our conversation with, "I was sad to hear about your classmate, Amelia Freeman. I know her parents. They must be devastated."

I told Dr. Reese that Amelia was my friend. Then I described the project we had been working on.

"Mrs. Simon, my English teacher, assigned me to work with Amelia, Barbara, and Gordon and we really hit it off. The day we brainstormed at my house was wonderful! The great ideas wouldn't stop coming. But it wasn't all serious. We had fun *and* worked well together. We joked and laughed right up to the time Amelia had to leave. Her family was going out to dinner. To try out some new restaurant."

My eyes widened and my throat suddenly went dry.

"Mary Anne?" Dr. Reese leaned forward. "What is it?"

"I just remembered something," I said, my voice barely above a whisper. "Amelia invited us to go out to dinner with her. We joked about her dad's Volkswagen being too small to carry all of us. But Amelia genuinely wanted us to come with her." I looked at Dr. Reese and shivered. "Do you think if we'd gone we would have been in that accident? Or do you think the accident would never have happened?"

Dr. Reese sighed. "Those are things we'll never know. And you only upset yourself worrying about them."

I set my empty cup on her wicker coffee table. "I didn't think about the dinner invitation until just this minute."

"There are so many 'what ifs' in this world," Dr. Reese said. "But don't start torturing yourself thinking you could have changed the outcome of things. What's past is past."

I sighed. "I guess you're right."

Dr. Reese picked up my cup and took it to the small sink by her microwave. "You were talking about Amelia . . ."

"Yes." My mind continued to replay the events of the last time I saw Amelia. "When Amelia was leaving my house, she turned and smiled at me. It was a special kind of smile between two people who really like each other. I remember thinking in that moment just how happy I was to be working with her." I looked down at my hands clasped in my lap. "I went to bed that night happy."

"The next day, you heard the news about Amelia," Dr. Reese said.

I nodded. "I couldn't believe it."

"How did you feel?"

I cocked my head, trying to be specific about my emotions. "Sad, of course. Shocked. And scared."

"Scared?"

"I suddenly felt like everything was a joke. Locking doors, being careful crossing streets — none of that was going to protect me." My voice grew louder and louder as I spoke. "I mean, if someone as wonderful as Amelia could get killed for no reason at all, then nobody is safe."

"You sound angry," Dr. Reese said. "How have you handled your anger?"

"Anger?" I blinked in surprise at Dr. Reese. "I haven't been angry. Kristy is the one who's been mad."

"What has she done about her anger?"

"At first she kind of pulled into herself," I said, remembering those days right after Amelia's death. "Which was unusual for Kristy. Of all of us, she seemed to be taking Amelia's death the hardest, even though I was closer to Amelia than she was. Kristy was acting so strange that I started worrying about her."

Dr. Reese nodded. "Mary Anne, the caregiver."

"I guess it helped me, too," I confessed, "because for awhile there I put my feelings aside, and only concentrated on Kristy."

122

"How is Kristy doing now?"

I shrugged. "Couldn't be better. She's back to her old Kristy-self, organizing our school's chapter of Students Against Driving Drunk. Which is also kind of weird. I mean, she seemed so devastated, but less than a month later, she's completely recovered."

"It makes sense to me," Dr. Reese said.

"It does? Why?"

"Well, as I remember from your descriptions of her, Kristy is a real 'can do' kind of person. If she sees a problem, she solves it."

"That's Kristy."

"You mentioned that Kristy didn't know Amelia as well as you did, and yet she was overwhelmed by her death."

"That's right."

Dr. Reese sat back on the chaise. "Kristy, being a problem solver, was suddenly hit with a problem she couldn't solve. One of her classmates was senselessly killed in a car accident and there was nothing she could do to change that."

I nodded. "She raved on and on about drunk drivers and how we should put them all behind bars."

Dr. Reese held out her hands. "Kristy finally found a way to channel her anger. She organized S.A.D.D. It wouldn't bring Amelia back, but it would help thousands of kids your age change things. In her own way, Kristy is keeping those drivers off the streets. She's avenging Amelia's death."

"But I helped Kristy form the club. I've been putting up posters and making phone calls. And I feel worse than ever."

"But your grief wasn't about controlling your life. It was about losing a friend."

I thought of Amelia looking back over her shoulder at me. "Yes, I did lose a friend." My chin started to quiver and big tears rolled down my cheeks. Then I began to sob. I could barely talk. "It's just so . . . *sad*," I whispered.

"Losing people we love *is* sad. It hurts," Dr. Reese said. "And it's okay to cry. For them and for ourselves."

When I left Dr. Reese's office that afternoon I felt as though my entire body had been put through a wringer. But at last I knew what was wrong with me. I was in mourning for my friend. And as Dr. Reese pointed out, that sorrow just doesn't disappear. It gradually lessens, but we have to allow ourselves time to grieve.

For the rest of the week, I did just that. I looked at my class picture of Amelia and my yearbook from seventh grade. As Dr. Reese had suggested, I kept an Amelia journal, writing down my memories of her. I remembered her winning a spelling bee in fifth grade. I remembered her tripping in the cafeteria and smearing an entire tray of spaghetti down the front of her white blouse. I remembered Amelia doing the flexed arm hang the longest in gym class — and fudging on the sit-ups.

On my next visit to Dr. Reese, I brought my journal.

"Excellent," Dr. Reese said. "You haven't turned her into some perfect girl, you've kept her human."

I flipped open the journal again. There were more empty pages than filled ones. And it somehow felt inadequate. "This has been a big help, because I was secretly afraid that I might forget Amelia." I leaned back in my chair and sighed. "I just wish there was something more I could do."

Dr. Reese once again made us hot chocolate. As she handed me my cup, she asked, "Have you considered doing something to publicly memorialize Amelia? Barbara, Josh, and other students who were close to her might want to help you."

"But we already had a funeral," I replied.

"Something more personal," Dr. Reese said. "Something just you and your friends would do."

I took a sip of my chocolate. "Barbara, Gordon, and I plan to dedicate our English project to Amelia."

"Something a bit bigger," Dr. Reese said gently. "Something that might allow Amelia's name or her memory to live on."

Hmm. I liked that idea. A lot. I left Dr. Reese's office feeling hopeful for the first time in a long while.

That night, I set to work collecting ideas for a way to memorialize Amelia. I called Dawn in California, then talked to Dad and Sharon.

Dad suggested we start a scholarship fund in Amelia's name.

Sharon thought we could put up a plaque at the school.

Dawn suggested we make donations to a green fund such as Save the Rain Forests, since Amelia was interested in ecology.

Everyone's ideas were good, but I decided I'd wait until the perfect one appeared. That night I went to bed feeling better than I had in weeks.

CHAPTER 13

Sunday

Dear Mary Anne,
    Three whole weeks
and not a peep out of
Mr. Cruickshank. It
was making me crazy.
We'd cleaned up the
trash, but what was
left was just a big old
dirt lot in the middle of
our beautiful neighbor-
hood. The kids were
growing antsy. They
wanted to plant a
garden. And so did I!

I'd had a feeling even before I opened the mailbox that I'd hear from Dawn. And sure enough, there was her letter, written on blue stationery. She'd used purple ink. The outside of the envelope was decorated with little hearts and moon stickers. I could tell the letter was going to be a good one.

It seems that Mr. Cruickshank never wrote back. Dawn had even written him two more letters after the first one. Finally she couldn't stand waiting anymore. She marched over to Sunny's house and rang the doorbell.

"The trash is gone, the weeds have been pulled, and the kids are standing by ready to plant a garden. We need to get going."

"It's making me crazy, too," Sunny said. "Maybe Mr. Cruickshank never read our letters. Maybe he was out of town."

"Maybe he read the letters, but couldn't care less about the lot," Dawn countered. "I mean, look how he let it become a trash heap."

"You think we should just go ahead and plant a garden?"

Dawn shrugged. "Why not? How mad could he be about a beautiful garden that didn't cost him a cent?"

"You're right," Sunny said. "Let's plant it."

Dawn and Sunny rallied the rest of the We ♥ Kids Club and, although they didn't feel quite right about their plan, they reminded each other that not three weeks before, the lot had been a health hazard and an eyesore. Their hard work was going to turn the ugliest spot in the neighborhood into the garden spot.

The group kicked into high gear. Many of the parents helped out by hauling things for them. This time it wasn't garbage; it was sacks of fertilizer, flats of plants, and bags of seeds. They even hauled wheelbarrowloads of pebbles.

"Now tell me once more why you need so many rocks?" Dawn's stepmother Carol asked as they stuffed her trunk with bags of gravel.

"For the walkways," Dawn explained. "You see, we drew up a garden plan. We want ours to be like the one in *The Secret Garden*. Where kids can walk through the lot and view the plants. We've even talked about adding a gazebo."

"A gazebo?" Carol gasped. "But won't that cost a lot of money?"

"Mr. Clune is donating it. He said he hadn't seen his girls so excited since Christmas. And he was glad that instead of focusing on presents, they were creating something beautiful."

"I have a friend who makes birdhouses," Carol remarked on their fifth trip across town. "Maybe I could convince her to donate a few."

"Oh, that would be wonderful!" Dawn cried. "Then we could put in a birdbath.

Stephie really wants a birdbath.''

It took the club, their clients, the kids, and several neighbors almost a week to collect the supplies they needed. But that gave the girls time to read a few gardening books and gather advice from their parents and local greenhouses.

Sunny drew the final design of the garden, and Maggie Blume, another of the We ♥ Kids Club members, copied them at her dad's office. Each little kid was given a design to color.

They were lucky the Green Thumb nursery decided to donate so many large plants and bushes. They transformed the dirt lot practically overnight.

It became a palette of pastels, with white alyssum, salmon-pink day lilies, pink geraniums, and purple petunias.

Some of the adults agreed to help put in the gravel walkways after everything was planted. By then, it was Sunday afternoon, and what started as a work party turned into a neighborhood celebration. Families brought lemonade and cookies, and everyone who had contributed to the garden showed up to watch the completion of the walkways.

Dawn had just taken a break and was standing next to Sunny, sipping a cup of lemonade, when a huge black car with tinted windows pulled up in front of the lot.

"Uh-oh," Dawn said, lowering her cup.

"Do you know who that is?" Sunny asked, following Dawn's gaze.

"No, but I can guess." Dawn crumpled her cup and tossed it into the metal can at the edge of the lot. "Mr. James L. Cruickshank."

Right on cue, the back door of the car swung open and a man in a three-piece suit and mirrored sunglasses stepped out.

"Does he look happy?" Sunny whispered to Dawn. "I don't think he looks happy."

"It's hard to tell anything," Dawn whispered back. "His sunglasses are hiding his eyes."

The man stood on the sidewalk and stared at his lot. He didn't smile. He didn't turn his head to acknowledge anyone. He just looked.

"I can't take it anymore," Dawn finally said to Sunny. "I'm going to talk to him."

Sunny grabbed Dawn's elbow. "Wait for me. I'm not letting you face that iceberg alone."

Dawn marched over to the man and said, "Mr. Cruickshank? I'm Dawn Schafer. I'm the one who wrote you all those letters."

The man slowly turned his head toward Dawn. He stared at her, his face absolutely expressionless, for a full minute. Finally he said, "I've been out of town."

"See? I told you," Sunny mumbled out of the corner of her mouth.

"I didn't have a chance to read my mail until this morning. That's why I'm here." He looked back at the lot. "But I guess I'm too late to stop this."

Dawn let out a nervous laugh. "I guess so. Unless you want us to dig up the plants and dump all that garbage back onto your lot."

Mr. Cruickshank shot her a stiff look, letting her know he did *not* appreciate the crack about the garbage.

"I mean, we can stop what we're doing," Dawn stammered. "If that's what you want."

The man stroked his chin. "I'm not sure what I want. I never had any real plans for this lot."

"Well, it makes a wonderful garden," Sunny piped up. "We've only been working a short while, and see how beautiful it is now? Imagine what it will look like when all the plants are in bloom."

Mr. Cruickshank turned and walked down the gravel paths. He occasionally stopped to study a tag still on a bush or shrub, but mostly he just walked. Very slowly.

"I think this is worse than waiting for his letter," Dawn murmured to Sunny. "Look at him — no smiles, no nothing. The guy has icewater in his veins."

132

"Shhh!" Sunny pressed her finger to her lips. "He might hear you."

"What's he going to do, sue me?" Dawn asked.

"No, but he could make us dig up that garden. And he could take us all to court for trespassing."

Dawn gasped in disbelief. "Are you sure?"

"Cross my heart." Sunny placed one hand on her heart and held up the other, palm outward.

"Well, if you knew that, why didn't you say something?" Dawn exploded. "Before we dug up the entire lot and did all of the planting?"

"Because I never thought he'd show up," Sunny retorted. "I mean, that lot looked like no one had gone near it in ten years."

The neighbors, thinking Mr. Cruickshank was just an interested passerby, continued their party, laughing and joking with each other.

"This could be a total embarrassment," Dawn murmured out of the side of her mouth. "He could throw a fit and we'd be forced to admit to all these parents that we didn't have permission to do this."

Sunny's eyes widened. "Did you tell them we did?"

"Well, I did and I didn't. Whenever anyone asked about it, I would tell them we'd written several letters to Mr. Cruickshank, the owner."

Sunny nodded slowly. "I see, and they'd *think* you had permission."

"Right."

Mr. Cruickshank was now walking in their direction.

"What should we do?" Dawn hissed. "Beg him to let us keep the garden?"

"Beg?" Sunny gasped. "We Winslows never beg. Plead, yes . . ."

"It appears you've done quite a bit of work here," Mr. Cruickshank said. "I must say, I'm extremely surprised."

Dawn couldn't tell if he was surprised that his lot could look so nice, or surprised that they would have the nerve to do so much without permission.

"I hope you like it," Sunny said, with a cheery smile. "We loved working on it."

Mr. Cruickshank took a deep breath and said sternly, "You realize that, no matter what you do to this lot, I am still the owner."

"Yes sir," both girls answered meekly.

"And all of these plants, bushes, and flowers are now *my* plants, bushes, and flowers."

They hadn't fully realized that but they nodded anyway.

"And as owner, I could choose to sell this lot tomorrow, and whoever bought it would

134

be the sole owner of this garden."

"Yes sir," they answered in even tinier voices.

"I could also come in here next week," he continued, "and bulldoze this lot and build a house on it."

The more they listened to Mr. Cruickshank, the more dismayed Dawn and Sunny felt. All of their hard work could be wiped out in a heartbeat.

"However." Mr. Cruickshank removed his sunglasses for the first time, revealing not the steely blue eyes they would have expected, but brown, almost warm, eyes. "At the moment I have no plans for this lot. So if you and your friends wish to continue to work on this garden . . ."

Dawn and Sunny held their breath.

"You have my permission."

After Mr. Cruickshank left, Dawn and Sunny realized they needed to tell the kids the truth. They gathered them together and Dawn explained the letter-writing process, ending with the conversation they had just had with Mr. Cruickshank.

Some of the kids were disappointed, but Stephie raised her hand. "I don't care if we only have our secret garden for one week. I've loved working on it."

"I'm not quitting," Erick DeWitt declared.

"I want to see my flowers bloom."

After a little more discussion, they took a vote, and every kid, mom, and dad present decided to continue with the project.

Dawn closed her letter sounding slightly let down by the adventure.

But I was thrilled. Dawn's letter had given me a terrific idea.

CHAPTER 14

Barbara. I had to call Barbara.

If she liked my idea, then I'd go ahead with it. I called her the second I finished Dawn's letter. She agreed to meet me before school the next morning. She also agreed to bring Josh Freeman with her.

My talks with Dr. Reese had helped me. I felt much more energetic and positive about the future. I was even excited, because I had finally thought of something I could do for my friend Amelia.

The next morning, I arrived at our meeting place early. I'd forgotten that it was still pretty cold outside. Just when my nose was starting to turn numb, Barbara and Josh arrived.

"Let's go inside," I said, my teeth chattering, "where it's warm."

When we got inside I asked, "What would you think of planting a garden at SMS in Amelia's memory?"

"I couldn't think of a more perfect memorial," Barbara said. "You know, *The Secret Garden* was Amelia's favorite movie."

"And she loved to garden," Josh added. He seemed genuinely happy, even though I could tell it was still difficult for him to talk about his sister. "Mom and Amelia planted a huge garden last year. One whole section was filled with flowers."

"Maybe we could even put up a plaque," I said, remembering Sharon's idea.

Barbara nodded eagerly. "That would be wonderful," she said.

"We could plant it near the front entrance of the school," I continued. "That way students who sit under the elm tree could sit in Amelia's garden."

"That would be the perfect spot," Barbara said. "What else could we put there besides flowers and a plaque?"

"A bench," Josh suggested.

Barbara and I looked at each other. "Perfect."

I felt tears starting to form in my eyes and took a deep breath, reminding myself that it was okay to grieve. I glanced at Josh and Barbara and saw they were both looking vulnerable, too.

The bell rang, snapping us back to the present.

138

"School," I said, making a face. "I forgot all about it."

Josh wiped at his eyes and smiled. "Me too."

"Why don't I talk to Mr. Seitz this morning?" I suggested as we headed toward the main hall. "He can let us know right away if this is even possible. Then I'll talk to you at lunchtime."

"I have a different lunchtime than you guys," Josh reminded me.

"Mary Anne can tell me the news," Barbara said. "And I'll pass it on to you, Josh."

"Cool." Josh gave Barbara a thumbs-up. I could tell Josh was excited about my idea, and that made me happy.

Mr. Seitz was all for the garden. "When the chips are down, you kids really come up with some great ideas." He shook his head in admiration. "I can't think of a nicer gift to give the Freeman family."

Mr. Seitz said he would check into using the area near the elm tree. "But I should warn you, there are a lot of people who have to sign off on this before it can happen — Mr. Taylor, our superintendent, the school board, and probably even our parent/teacher group."

For the next few weeks, Josh, Barbara, and I were on pins and needles. All of the school officials liked the idea but they couldn't agree on the location. The biology teacher pointed out that a garden wouldn't be much of a garden under the shade of the huge elm tree, so we began to search for other spots on the school grounds.

Barbara liked the idea of a garden outside the cafeteria window, but that would have meant removing some asphalt from one of the basketball courts.

The teachers, students, and even parents submitted ideas for a location, but still no decision could be made.

Finally, one evening, I got a phone call from Mr. Seitz.

"We found the spot," he said excitedly.

"That's great!" I shouted into the phone.

"I've just lost all hearing in my left ear," Mr. Seitz said with a laugh.

"Where is it?" I asked, after apologizing for shouting.

"It's not under the elm or outside the cafeteria," Mr. Seitz said. "But frankly, I think this spot is even better. What do you think of the courtyard?"

"The courtyard!" I gasped. "That would be wonderful."

The courtyard is a sunny open spot in the middle of SMS. It's a place where students can meet to chat. It's also a nice place just to sit and think. It was perfect, and I wondered why we hadn't thought of it before.

Because it was still winter, we couldn't start the planting yet. But we could begin fund-raising for supplies. I remembered Dawn's efforts and suggested we not buy any gardening tools, but ask kids to bring them from home. (Clearly labeled, of course.)

We jumped ahead with plans for a dedication.

"Once the site has officially been approved by SMS," Mr. Seitz suggested, "then I think we should hold a public groundbreaking ceremony. Let's shoot for two weeks from today."

Goosebumps had appeared on my arms. I hung up the phone and shouted into the kitchen where Dad and Sharon were having dessert, "It's going to happen. The garden is actually going to happen."

Then I dialed Barbara and squealed, "We've got the land! Amelia's going to have her garden."

Barbara answered me by exclaiming, "I've found a donor for the bench!"

I couldn't help myself. I shouted, "All right!"

After we'd finished our call, I collapsed on the living room rug. At long last, everything was falling into place.

CHAPTER 15

"S un?"

I blinked my eyes at the unfamiliar glare. I wasn't dreaming. It actually was sunlight streaming through my window.

"Yes!"

It was almost as if winter had ended and spring had arrived. I leaped out of bed, and almost clicked my heels as I hurried to my closet.

Today was a very big day. Even though it was still winter, I decided to wear something light and spring-like. After all, this memorial service wasn't a funeral. It was a celebration of Amelia. Pure and simple.

I think Claud and Stacey had been hit with the same feeling, because when I spotted them on the corner, standing in the yellow morning sun, they looked like an advertisement for spring wear from some very trendy boutique.

"I have sensational news!" Claud cried as I ran to join them.

"Let me guess," I said. "You won the lottery and you are splitting it with the BSC."

"Better news than that." Claudia was beaming. "Peaches is pregnant."

"What? Claud, that's wonderful!" I threw my arms around her in a big hug.

Peaches is Claudia's favorite aunt. She and her husband have been trying for years to have a baby. She did get pregnant once, which is why they moved to Stoneybrook, but then she had a miscarriage. It was a very sad time for Peaches and the Kishi family.

"When did you hear?" I asked.

"Last night," Claud replied. "She and Russ wanted to wait awhile before telling anyone. She's nearly six months pregnant and the doctor says the baby is in perfect health."

"Oh, Claud," I said, "that is such great news."

I don't know what it was — the warm sunlight, or just the feeling that spring had finally arrived — but Claud, Stacey, and I did something we hadn't done in ages.

We looped arms and did the "We're off to see the Wizard!" skip all the way to school.

The service was scheduled for the end of the school day. In fact, Mr. Kingbridge had agreed to release the students one hour early.

I spent most of the day out of class. There was so much to do. Because there wasn't enough room for everyone in the courtyard, the microphone and podium were to be set up on the front steps of the school. A beautiful flower garland had to be hung across the school entrance. Donor forms needed to be strategically placed in boxes around the school grounds.

Judging from the turnout at the funeral, we had figured we'd better prepare for hundreds and hundreds of people.

We were right.

About a half an hour before the ceremony was to start, cars started arriving. The parking lot filled up in seconds, and soon every space on the street bordering the school was taken.

Five minutes before the service began, the Freemans, our guests of honor, took their places in the chairs surrounding the podium. Mrs. Freeman was wearing the pink rose corsage we'd given her, and she was smiling.

During the entire week before the ceremony Barbara and I had gone back and forth about who should make the speech dedicating the ground.

"You should do it," Barbara had insisted. "After all, it was your idea."

"No way." Just thinking about making a

speech in front of hundreds of people made my stomach churn and my head feel woozy. "You should do it. You were Amelia's best friend."

Finally we reached a compromise.

"I'll stand in the front row by the podium," I said. That way Logan, Kristy, and the rest of my friends from the Baby-sitters Club could stand with me.

The dedication ceremony began. First our principal, Mr. Taylor, welcomed the guests to Stoneybrook Middle School. The P.A. system broadcast the speeches across the schoolgrounds where hundreds of students stood listening.

Mr. Seitz spoke next, introducing the man who was responsible for giving the final okay on the garden, our superintendent of schools.

The superintendent's speech was brief. "We're proud to be able to support this very worthy project. I've known the Freemans since they first moved to Stoneybrook and I felt their pain when they lost Amelia. Now, thanks to you students, Amelia's memory can live on."

When Barbara took the podium, she brought an eight-by-ten photo with her. "This is my best friend Amelia and her rabbit, Nibs," Barbara began.

Barbara talked about how Amelia had loved SMS, and how much the memorial garden would have meant to her. She thanked the Berkhoff family for the donation of the bench, and talked about the plaque.

"Next week the bench with Amelia's plaque will be delivered and installed on the garden site. And in May we will begin landscaping and planting," Barbara said.

Applause filled the air.

"And now, Josh Freeman would like to say a few words."

I had been holding up pretty well during most of the ceremony, but the sight of Josh, looking so earnest and young, brought me to tears.

Mr. and Mrs. Freeman stood on either side of their son as he made his short speech.

"My family would like to thank the school board, Stoneybrook Middle School, and the Berkhoffs for their generous donations. And we would like to express our special love and thanks to Mary Anne Spier for thinking of this idea in the first place."

There was more applause. Josh smiled at me and, even though my face was burning, I managed to smile back.

"And Barbara Hirsch, for helping to make it happen."

Barbara, who had taken her seat behind the podium, waved to Josh and the crowd.

"In closing I would like to thank someone

who can't be here to accept your applause," Josh said. "Someone who was always willing to listen when I needed to talk. Someone who made sure I was included in her friends' games. Someone who was never ashamed to tell me she loved me."

I clutched Logan's hand so hard, my nails dug into his skin.

"I'd like to thank my sister." Josh turned to his parents, who were smiling proudly through their tears. "We love you, Amelia. And we will always miss you."

I cried. I think everyone did.

After the ceremony ended, Logan walked me home. I was finally at peace. Dr. Reese would have said that I had reached closure.

I was planning to see Dr. Reese one more time, mostly to let her know about our garden, and to thank her for helping me sort things out.

To make the day perfect, a postcard from Dawn was waiting for me when I arrived home.

Friday

Dear Mary Anne,
♫ Ta-ra-ra-boom-de-ay, we got the land today! ♫
Can you believe it?
Stephie Robertson and

147

I were working in the garden pulling weeds (yup, we already have weeds) when who should appear but Mr. "Iceberg" Cruickshank. He cruised up in his land yacht and just sat there with the engine running. For a minute I thought he was going to take the garden away from us for good. Apparently he was just waiting to see if we were really going to follow through with the garden. When he saw everything in bloom, and Stephie digging away in her oversized garden gloves, he just melted. Within minutes, the lot was ours. Hooray!

your not-so-secret
gardener,
Dawn

A Note to Readers

If you are interested in learning more about
Students Against Driving Drunk, please
write to:

S.A.D.D.
P.O. Box 800
Marlboro, MA 01752

Dear Reader:

Every year I receive 15,000 letters from readers of the Baby-sitters Club books. Over the years I have received many letters requesting a story dealing with the death of a classmate. The letters were from kids who had experienced this themselves and thought that reading about the subject might make them and others feel better. I had also received letters about the problem of drunk driving. And so this was the beginning of *Mary Anne and the Memory Garden*.

Some kids told me that they wanted to find a meaningful way to remember the person they had lost, but didn't know what to do. This is the problem Mary Anne experiences in the book. Several years ago, when friends of mine died tragically, people close to them got together and decided to remember them with a project that eventually became the Lisa Novak Libraries. People throughout the country donate new books to be sorted into libraries for children. A memorial doesn't have to be quite that big; it can be as simple as a scrapbook, or a garden like Mary Anne's. People may leave, but memories live on forever.

Ann M Martin

Ann M. Martin

About the Author

ANN MATTHEWS MARTIN was born on August 12, 1955. She grew up in Princeton, NJ, with her parents and her younger sister, Jane.

Although Ann used to be a teacher and then an editor of children's books, she's now a full-time writer. She gets the ideas for her books from many different places. Some are based on personal experiences. Others are based on childhood memories and feelings. Many are written about contemporary problems or events.

All of Ann's characters, even the members of the Baby-sitters Club, are made up. (So is Stoneybrook.) But many of her characters are based on real people. Sometimes Ann names her characters after people she knows, other times she chooses names she likes.

In addition to the Baby-sitters Club books, Ann Martin has written many other books for children. Her favorite is *Ten Kids, No Pets* because she loves big families and she loves animals. Her favorite Baby-sitters Club book is *Kristy's Big Day*. (By the way, Kristy is her favorite baby-sitter!)

Ann M. Martin now lives in New York with her cats, Gussie and Woody. Her hobbies are reading, sewing, and needlework — especially making clothes for children.

THE BABY-SITTERS CLUB

Notebook Pages

This Baby-sitters Club book belongs to _____ .

I am _____ years old and in the _____

grade.

The name of my school is _____ .

I got this BSC book from _____ .

I started reading it on _____ and

finished reading it on _____ .

The place where I read most of this book is _____ .

My favorite part was when _____ .

If I could change anything in the story, it might be the part when

_____ .

My favorite character in the Baby-sitters Club is _____ .

The BSC member I am most like is _____

because _____ .

If I could write a Baby-sitters Club book it would be about _____

_____ .

#93 Mary Anne and the Memory Garden

Mary Anne will really miss Amelia Freeman. One person I really

miss is _____ .

The things I miss the most about this person are _____

_____

_____ . Mary Anne and the other

Baby-sitters Club members are glad they will have their memories

of Amelia forever. The happiest memory I have of someone who

is gone is _____

_____

_____ . Mary Anne will always think

of Amelia when she passes by the memory garden. A good way

to remember someone is _____

_____

_____ . If I could say one thing to someone I don't

see anymore, it would be _____

_____ .

MARY ANNE'S

Party girl -- age 4

Sitting for the Pikes is always an adventure

Sitting for Andrea and Jenny Prezzioso -- a quiet moment.

SCRAPBOOK

*Logan and me.
Summer luv at Sea City.*

Illustrations by Angelo Tillery

*My family--
Jeff, Dad and Sharon,
Dawn and me and Tigger.*

Read all the books
about **Mary Anne**
in the Baby-sitters Club series
by Ann M. Martin

Look for #94

STACEY McGILL, SUPER SITTER

Greed. It's a dangerous thing.

That's what I was thinking the following Wednesday as I ran around the Cheplins' house like a total maniac trying to accomplish Mrs. Cheplin's ever-growing list of things to be done.

How I'd come to dread that list. I even had nightmares about it. The night before, I'd dreamt that I was walking home from school with Robert, and Mrs. Cheplin walked right behind us telling me all the things she wanted done in a steady stream of chatter. And, in my dream, her chores were even worse than in real life. "Stacey, paint the house, wash the windows, patch all the clothes, do the grocery shopping, fix the roof, cook a lasagna." In the dream I covered my ears and tried to get away from her but she chased me, rambling on about her list all the while. "Wallpaper the living room, carpet the stairs, get rid of my clutter, cure Dana's diabetes."

That's when I woke up. "I can't!" I cried, still half in my dream. Then I woke up fully and realized I was in my bedroom. I was glad to be out of *that* dream.

But I wanted the money. Was that greed? In a way, it was. Because I now no longer only wanted to take Robert to Broadway. Now I wanted to take him somewhere fancy for dinner. I also wanted to buy a new dress, something that would really look special for this special night.

THE BABY-SITTERS CLUB®

by Ann M. Martin

More titles... ▶

The Baby-sitters Club titles continued...

❑ MG47011-6	#73 Mary Anne and Miss Priss	$3.50
❑ MG47012-4	#74 Kristy and the Copycat	$3.50
❑ MG47013-2	#75 Jessi's Horrible Prank	$3.50
❑ MG47014-0	#76 Stacey's Lie	$3.50
❑ MG48221-1	#77 Dawn and Whitney, Friends Forever	$3.50
❑ MG48222-X	#78 Claudia and Crazy Peaches	$3.50
❑ MG48223-8	#79 Mary Anne Breaks the Rules	$3.50
❑ MG48224-6	#80 Mallory Pike, #1 Fan	$3.50
❑ MG48225-4	#81 Kristy and Mr. Mom	$3.50
❑ MG48226-2	#82 Jessi and the Troublemaker	$3.50
❑ MG48235-1	#83 Stacey vs. the BSC	$3.50
❑ MG48228-9	#84 Dawn and the School Spirit War	$3.50
❑ MG48236-X	#85 Claudi Kishi, Live from WSTO	$3.50
❑ MG48227-0	#86 Mary Anne and Camp BSC	$3.50
❑ MG48237-8	#87 Stacey and the Bad Girls	$3.50
❑ MG22872-2	#88 Farewell, Dawn	$3.50
❑ MG22873-0	#89 Kristy and the Dirty Diapers	$3.50
❑ MG45575-3	Logan's Story Special Edition Readers' Request	$3.25
❑ MG47118-X	Logan Bruno, Boy Baby-sitter Special Edition Readers' Request	$3.50
❑ MG47756-0	Shannon's Story Special Edition	$3.50
❑ MG44240-6	Baby-sitters on Board! Super Special #1	$3.95
❑ MG44239-2	Baby-sitters' Summer Vacation Super Special #2	$3.95
❑ MG43973-1	Baby-sitters' Winter Vacation Super Special #3	$3.95
❑ MG42493-9	Baby-sitters' Island Adventure Super Special #4	$3.95
❑ MG43575-2	California Girls! Super Special #5	$3.95
❑ MG43576-0	New York, New York! Super Special #6	$3.95
❑ MG44963-X	Snowbound Super Special #7	$3.95
❑ MG44962-X	Baby-sitters at Shadow Lake Super Special #8	$3.95
❑ MG45661-X	Starring the Baby-sitters Club Super Special #9	$3.95
❑ MG45674-1	Sea City, Here We Come! Super Special #10	$3.95
❑ MG47015-9	The Baby-sitter's Remember Super Special #11	$3.95
❑ MG48308-0	Here Come the Bridesmaids Super Special #12	$3.95

Available wherever you buy books...or use this order form.

Scholastic Inc., P.O. Box 7502, 2931 E. McCarty Street, Jefferson City, MO 65102

Please send me the books I have checked above. I am enclosing $ _____
(please add $2.00 to cover shipping and handling). Send check or money order—no
cash or C.O.D.s please.

Name _____ Birthdate _____

Address _____

City _____ State/Zip _____

Please allow four to six weeks for delivery. Offer good in the U.S. only. Sorry, mail orders are not
available to residents of Canada. Prices subject to change.

BSC395

What's the scoop with Dawn, Kristy, Mallory, and the other girls?

Be the first to know with G★I★R★L★ magazine!

Hey, Baby-sitters Club readers! Now you can be the first on the block to get in on the action of G★I★R★L★ It's an exciting new magazine that lets you dig in and read...

★ Upcoming selections from Ann Martin's Baby-sitters Club books
★ Fun articles on handling stress, turning dreams into great careers, making and keeping best friends, and much more
★ Plus, all the latest on new movies, books, music, and sports!

To get in on the scoop, just cut and mail this coupon today. And don't forget to tell all your friends about G★I★R★L★ magazine!

A neat offer for you...6 issues for only $15.00.

Sign up today -- this special offer ends July 1, 1996!

❑ **YES!** Please send me G★I★R★L★ magazine. I will receive six fun-filled issues for only $15.00. Enclosed is a check (no cash, please) made payable to G★I★R★L★ for $15.00.

Just fill in, cut out, and mail this coupon with your payment of $15.00 to: G★I★R★L★, c/o Scholastic Inc., 2931 East McCarty Street, Jefferson City, MO 65101.

Name _____

Address _____

City, State, ZIP _____

9013